Such a Pretty Girl

"In the magnetic latest from Greenwood, a former child actor faces her childhood traumas after a photo of her is found in the collection of an alleged pedophile . . . In Ryan's introspective narration, she explores her mother's betrayal and quest for self-gratification, and her determination to offer her own daughter a different kind of life. This knotty story leaves readers reflecting on the limits of family obligations."
—*Publishers Weekly*

Keeping Lucy

"A baby born less than perfect in the world's eyes, a mother persuaded that giving up her child is for the best, a lingering bond that pulls and tugs yet will not break. *Keeping Lucy* follows a mother willing to give up everything to save the child she's been told she must forget. This story will have readers not only rooting for Ginny and Lucy, but thinking about them long after the last page is turned." —Lisa Wingate, *New York Times* bestselling author of *Before We Were Yours*

Grace

"Exceptionally well-observed. Readers who enjoy insightful and sensitive family drama (Lionel Shriver's *We Need to Talk About Kevin*; Rosellen Brown's *Before and After*) will appreciate discovering Greenwood." —*Library Journal*

Breathing Water

"A poignant, clear-eyed first novel . . . filled with careful poetic description . . . the story is woven skillfully."
—*The New York Times Book Review*

"A poignant debut . . . Greenwood sensitively and painstakingly unravels her protagonist's self-loathing and replaces it with a graceful dignity." —*Publishers Weekly*

"A vivid, somberly engaging first book." —Larry McMurtry

The Season of
Second Chances

Books by Kristina McMorris

LETTERS FROM HOME*
BRIDGE OF SCARLET LEAVES*
THE PIECES WE KEEP*
THE EDGE OF LOST*
SOLD ON A MONDAY
THE WAYS WE HIDE

Books by Tammy Greenwood

THE STILL POINT*
SUCH A PRETTY GIRL*
TWO RIVERS*
THE HUNGRY SEASON*
UNDRESSING THE MOON*
THIS GLITTERING WORLD*
NEARER THAN THE SKY*
GRACE*
BREATHING WATER*
BODIES OF WATER*
THE FOREVER BRIDGE*
WHERE I LOST HER*
THE GOLDEN HOUR*
KEEPING LUCY
RUST & STARDUST

*Published by Kensington Publishing Corp.

The Season of Second Chances

KRISTINA MCMORRIS

TAMMY GREENWOOD

KENSINGTON
PUBLISHING CORP.

www.kensingtonbooks.com

KENSINGTON BOOKS are published by

Kensington Publishing Corp.
119 West 40th Street
New York, NY 10018

All Kensington titles, imprints, and distributed lines are available at special quantity discounts for bulk purchases for sales promotion, premiums, fund-raising, educational, or institutional use.

This book is a work of fiction. Names, characters, businesses, organizations, places, events, and incidents either are the product of the author's imagination or are used fictitiously. Any resemblance to actual persons, living or dead, events, or locales is entirely coincidental.

To the extent that the image or images on the cover of this book depict a person or persons, such person or persons are merely models, and are not intended to portray any character or characters featured in the book.

Special book excerpts or customized printings can also be created to fit specific needs. For details, write or phone the office of the Kensington Sales Manager: Kensington Publishing Corp., 119 West 40th Street, New York, NY 10018. Attn. Sales Department. Phone: 1-800-221-2647.

The K with book logo Reg US Pat. & TM Off.

ISBN: 978-1-4967-4423-4 (ebook)

ISBN: 978-1-4967-4422-7

First Kensington Trade Paperback Printing: September 2023

10 9 8 7 6 5 4 3 2 1

Printed in the United States of America

Contents

The Christmas Collector

KRISTINA MCMORRIS

Chapter 1

She tried to ignore him throughout dinner, but the squatty monk held Jenna's focus in a fisted grip. He mocked her with a half smile curled into round rosy cheeks, his hand resting on the wide shelf of his belly. Traditionally a symbol of self-sacrifice and frugality, he instead radiated sheer overindulgence.

The fact he was a mere saltshaker didn't lessen Jenna Matthews's anxiety. She shifted in her seat, forced down another bite of instant mashed potatoes. She knew without question the Friar Tuck collectible was new to her mother's house. In a brown robe, his hair forming a silver wreath, he stood amid the Thanksgiving dishes as if staking his claim. A matching pepper shaker and sugar bowl flanked him on the dining room table. Candlelight flickered over the trio, casting shadows across the floral vase and oval doily.

New vase. New doily. New condiment holders. All signs that Jenna's mother, Rita, had potentially relapsed.

But the woman gave no other indications. Over their holiday meal of turkey TV dinners—her mom's standard menu, now accustomed to cooking for one—she was rattling on about a film she had seen with a friend from her days in group therapy. Jenna feared those sessions might now be needed again.

"I just don't know why they insist on doing that." Her mother used a melodramatic tone for emphasis. "It ruins a perfectly good movie, don't you think?"

At the expectant pause, Jenna reviewed the discussion she had caught in disjointed pieces. "What does?"

"When they have those corny endings."

"Oh. Right."

"I swear, I can't recall the last time I saw a romantic comedy with a realistic ending. Some character always has to give an over-the-top speech in front of a reception hall, or even a whole baseball stadium. As if big revelations only come when you're holding a microphone." She shook her head, jostling her hoop earrings. "Honestly. When have you ever seen that happen in real life?"

Forging a smile, Jenna shrugged, and her mother moved on to the next topic: a Thanksgiving conspiracy by U.S. turkey farmers, based on her doubts over the pilgrims' actual supper. From a marketing perspective, Jenna hated to admit, the theory was intriguing enough to contemplate. She tried her best to listen, but her surroundings were of greater concern.

What other new purchases lurked in the shadows? She wrestled down the urge to spring from her chair and tear through the china cabinet on a hunt for more evidence. Perhaps she was overreacting.

Then again, she had witnessed firsthand how quickly a handful of knickknacks could multiply until they packed an entire mantel. A wall of bookshelves. Every drawer and cupboard in the house. And before long, you were drowning in a sea of objects no more satisfying than cotton candy: a temporary filler that, for her mother, eventually gave way to the reality of loss. It was this very emptiness that had devoured most of Jenna's high school years.

"Honey?" her mother said.

"Sorry—what?"

"I was wondering what you wanted for Christmas this year."

"*Nothing.*" The reply came stronger than intended. "I mean . . . there really isn't anything I need."

"Well, then. I'll just have to get creative." She flashed a smile, accentuating the Mary Kay lipstick she'd worn since the early nineties. Her shimmery eye shadow matched her irises, a deep sea green like Jenna's, and created arcs under brown bangs teased to a frizz. Only once had Jenna tried to update her mom's fashion, citing her cowl neck sweater and stirrup pants, like the ones she wore now, as "Goodwill bound." The half joke didn't fly. Her mother had licked her wounds by buying six new bags of useless "stuff."

Of course, that was back in the midst of her mom's grieving, too soon after their family of three became two. Maybe, at last, she would consider a small change.

"I was thinking," Jenna began, gauging her approach, "I should probably get my hair colored in the next few weeks."

"Oh?" her mother said. "Are you going with a different shade?"

"Just getting rid of the gray." Jenna's stylist would faint from joy if Jenna ever agreed to liven up her shaggy brown bob with red or blond highlights, rather than simply masking her scatterings of early silver. "Why don't you come along? Maybe try taking off a couple inches. You know, you'd look great with short hair."

Her mother's expression perked for a moment, the idea like a sun rising, then just as swiftly setting. She smoothed the ends of her shoulder-length do. "Maybe some other time."

At thirty-one, Jenna knew that answer well. Through decades of asking permission—hosting a slumber party, buying over-priced jeans—the meaning hadn't changed. *Maybe some other time* equaled *No*.

Jenna returned to her shriveled, gravy-drenched stuffing. The wall clock ticked slowly away. Every swing of its pendulum echoed against the marred wooden floors.

And from the table, that ceramic friar kept right on staring. His painted eyes speared her thoughts, piercing the walls guarding her past. Despite her efforts, Jenna couldn't hold back. "When did you get the new saltshaker?"

"Huh? Ahh, that." Her mother brushed her hand clean with a napkin, monogrammed with an *L* for its previous owner—whoever that was—before picking up the item. "I got it back in, gosh, August I suppose. Apparently the creamer broke years ago. I thought I'd shown these to you already."

Jenna shook her head, bracing herself against her mother's nonchalance. Minor cracks and chips on the rims made the set's origin clear. A garage sale. Fliers and posters Jenna had passed on the drive here, each tacked to utility poles in the suburban Oregon neighborhood, now sprang to mind: *Yard sale this way! Clothes and furniture sale one block ahead!* They were like neon tavern signs tempting a recovering alcoholic.

Jenna should have visited more often, to keep better watch. With Christmas around the corner, folks everywhere loved purging their old junk to make room for new junk. It was the all-American way. As an estate liquidator, Jenna had built a career upon that very principle. But that didn't stop her from despising the holiday that brimmed with manufactured, assembly-line cheer.

As her mother gazed in admiration at the figurine, Jenna's insides twisted into a braid of fear. "I thought you stopped buying those kinds of things."

"Oh, no, I didn't buy—" Her mother's cheery tone dissolved as she explained, "It was from Aunt Lenore."

Aunt Lenore?

And then Jenna remembered. Over the summer, back in the Midwest, the youngest sister of Jenna's late grandmother had passed away. Lenore used to send them handwritten Christmas cards, among the few people who did that anymore, and create doilies to raise money for the food bank.

Doilies, like the one on the dinner table. The faded floral vase, too, must have belonged to her great aunt.

"So, you just inherited these things," Jenna realized. Relief washed through her until she met her mother's gaze, and a mixture of embarrassment and distrust ricocheted between them.

Jenna sank into her chair, weighted by guilt. She sipped her merlot while her mother set down the shaker. Silence returned, heavy as a damp blanket. It draped the black lacquered chairs, a fake fern in the corner, the framed photo tacked to a pinstriped wall. The black-and-white image caught Jenna's eye. In a grassy field stood a single tulip, almost three-dimensional, airbrushed in vibrant yellow.

"Did you snap that one?" she diverted.

Her mom looked over and nodded. "I was driving past a farm over in Damascus when I saw it. Just had to pull over."

"It's a really beautiful picture." A genuine compliment. Her mom's new job at a portrait studio, after a long career with the school district, had recently revived the hobby. "I like the color effect you added."

"Well, I did have some help with that part." A hint of excitement suddenly buoyed her voice. "I used this amazing new editing program. And Doobie's been wonderful, walking me through it. You remember me telling you about him?"

"A little." How could Jenna forget? The name of her mom's coworker sounded like a product of Woodstock. Or at least the remnants of what was smoked by everyone there.

"Anyway, he's also been teaching me about different lenses, and about the shutter speed for action shots—which has actually come in handy lately, with all the families getting their pictures taken for Christmas."

Given the modern rage of posting and sending digital images, Jenna was surprised families still bothered with formal portraits. Especially since, in reality, the majority of those mass-printed cards would receive a two-second glance before being tossed in a box.

Box . . .

Pictures . . .

Jenna groaned.

"What's wrong, honey?"

"I forgot to do something."

Terrence, her right-hand man on the current sale, had phoned her yesterday while boarding a plane to see family. "Promise me you'll grab it, so it doesn't land in the trash." He'd meant to set aside a box, which he suspected the client would want to keep.

While Jenna cared little about personal valuables, she did care about promises.

"I'd better get home," she told her mom. "I have to go to work early tomorrow." Early enough to beat Mrs. Porter's garbage truck.

"But it's Thanksgiving. I thought everyone else had the weekend off."

True, each of her four crew members did. Yet Jenna had the most to gain if they met their profit goal. And the most to lose if they failed.

"No rest for the weary, right?" she replied lightly. Feeling a tinge of regret, she averted her eyes while bundling up in her coat. "Thanks for dinner," she said as they walked to the entry.

"Are we still on for this weekend?" her mother pressed.

It took Jenna a moment to identify the reference: the last Sunday of the month, their standing lunch date.

"Absolutely."

They met in a brief hug before Jenna dashed outside and into the rain. Once seated in her car, she looked back at the house. Blue shutters, trimmed lawn, windows aglow. It was an image ideal for a mass-printed card.

From a distance.

Chapter 2

Drawing a deep breath of night air, Reece Porter rubbed his temples. Tension had formed an unbreakable knot. From a patio chair, he watched raindrops puddle on the tarp covering the pool. A drain spout drizzled a stream that bounced off the awning overhead, muted by the din of laughter and chatter and holiday tunes from inside the house.

He'd once considered the stereotypes of huge Italian families as nothing more than myth—pasta and red-sauce obsessed, talking over each other, involved in everyone's business—until he experienced his girlfriend's family, the Graniellos. Even the protectiveness exhibited by Tracy's brothers was fitting of a mob flick. When the accident happened two Decembers back, their distrust of Reece had magnified tenfold. But gradually he had earned their respect. In fact, aided by his dark features, few onlookers would guess he wasn't a natural link in the family circle.

He just wished that circle tonight didn't resemble a tightening vice.

Checking his watch, he blew out a sigh. Ten after nine. Another twenty minutes or so and he could excuse himself without being rude.

"There you are."

Reece turned toward the high yet gentle voice and found Tracy stepping outside, onto her parents' patio. He started to rise, a reflexive habit from months of helping her through doors, up flights of stairs. But she had already closed the sliding glass door on her own.

She held up a pair of steaming coffee mugs. "Hot Apple Pie or Peppermint Patty?"

The concoctions from her bartender cousin were always a little too sweet, but if nothing else, Reece enjoyed the tradition of them. He'd come to appreciate predictable comfort.

"I'll take whichever one you don't want."

After a pause, she shrugged a shoulder and gave him the one that smelled like cider. Then she smoothed her fitted dress and sat next to him. He blew on the surface and took a sip, only confirming his stomach's disinterest. The celebratory champagne was still swishing in his gut.

"You okay?" she asked.

"Yeah. Yeah, I'm fine. Just needed a little break from the noise is all."

She smiled in understanding. The contrast of his own family went without saying.

"You didn't eat much," Tracy remarked, and took a drink from her mug.

"Guess I'm still jet-lagged." It had been only five days since his return from a six-week stint in London, where he'd helped a top account implement a new order-tracking system as part of his global logistics job. On the way back he'd stopped through the San Francisco office and had flown back to Portland only this morning.

Perhaps travel weariness was the real root of the evening's claustrophobia. Or at least what was intensifying the pressure.

"You're up next, buddy," one of the uncles had told him

over dessert, after Tracy's sister had announced her engagement. Reece had grown well accustomed to the group-wide sentiment. So why did the comment feel more like a threat than an invitation? More importantly, after all he and Tracy had been through together, why were doubts about their future scratching at his mind?

Just look at the girl: perfect posture, as much from Catholic school as from years of riding equestrian; long black hair in a braid, highlighting her narrow features; gorgeous blue eyes, so light they were almost clear. She was no less striking than when they had first met at a charity golf scramble two summers ago. A petite thing, she'd instantly impressed him by nailing the longest drive on the third hole, all to raise funds for a new ward at St. Vincent's.

Little had Reece known how many hours he'd later spend at that very hospital, helping Tracy through physical therapy. The grueling sessions had sealed their bond. Yet that bond was no match for the discomfort now festering between them.

"So . . ." she said as if fishing for a topic. "Did you talk to your parents yet? To wish them a good Thanksgiving?"

"I called Grandma's, but nobody answered. So I left a message on my mom's cell."

"That's strange they weren't there." She was right, though there wasn't anywhere else they'd have spent the day.

"I'm sure they just missed the ring. I'll try again on my way home."

"I hope everything's all right."

Her tone caused Reece a niggling of concern. Elderly couples too often passed in pairs. Granted, it had been five years since losing his grandfather, and still, even at eighty-seven, his grandma was a healthy, feisty little thing.

Detouring from the thought, he mustered enthusiasm over the subject he had no logical reason to avoid. "That's great news, by the way, about Gabby."

Tracy returned his smile. "They make a great couple."

"Do they know where they're getting married?"

"They're talking about Sonoma, at the winery where they met. In the very spot he proposed."

Reece nodded, pushing himself to continue. "Have they set a date?"

"Gabby was hoping for a summer wedding, but Mom wants her to wait till Heidi has her baby, so traveling will be easier."

For a moment, Reece had forgotten Tracy's sister-in-law was expecting a second child. He tried for a casual comment, yet the words wouldn't flow, stopped by a barricade of milestones everyone around them was tackling with gusto.

He forced down another sip of his spiked cider. Beside him, Tracy fidgeted with the handle on her mug. Noise from the house lightened along with the rain, amplifying their exchange of quiet.

At last, she angled her body toward him. "Reece, I think it's time we talked. About our relationship."

He replied with forged levity. "What's on your mind?"

"The thing is, I've been giving my life a lot of thought while you were away. I'm almost thirty, and every time I try to envision us five or ten years down the road, nothing seems clear."

Without her saying it, he knew the source of the haze. It was him. What he didn't know was which obstacle continued to hold him back. From skydiving to bungee jumping, he used to be the type to literally plunge headfirst without a thought.

In a single day, all that had changed.

"I can't help but wonder," she went on, "if you're still with me just because—"

"Tracy!" a voice hollered from behind. Her mother had reopened the sliding glass door. "Heidi and Marco have been looking for you."

"They're not leaving yet, are they?"

"Marco said he wants to get up before dawn. He's already warming up the car."

Tracy let out a heavy breath. Apparently, she'd agreed to watch their toddler, freeing the couple for the Black Friday stampede. Not even pregnancy could deter shoppers on a mission.

She looked at Reece, clearly torn.

"Come on, come on," Tracy's mother urged. "They're waiting."

Reece gave Tracy's hand a tender squeeze. "Go ahead," he assured her. "We'll talk later."

Though hesitant, she nodded her agreement. He leaned over and kissed her on the lips, brief enough for a parental audience, and watched Tracy step inside. Her mother sent him an approving wave.

Alone again, he realized he, too, was now free to leave. Back in his apartment, he could better prepare for the rest of their discussion.

Before he could stand, his cell phone buzzed in his jacket pocket. He answered and found relief at the absence of urgency in his mother's tone.

"I'm sorry we didn't call you back earlier. Dinner had me going a bit crazy."

"How'd it turn out?"

"Not the best," she admitted wearily. "I tried to deep fry the turkey this year, and it was a total disaster. While I was dealing with *that* mess, half the side dishes ended up overcooked."

The kitchen always tended to be chaotic when, on the alternate years, his grandmother didn't run the show. But usually his sister provided damage control.

"Wasn't Lisa there to help?"

"She got stuck in terrible traffic in Seattle, so she didn't get here till late."

Reece felt a tug of regret for not joining them. Last year, he and Tracy had split time between both families and ended up not enjoying either one on a tight schedule. Now, at his mother's recap, he was struck by the family traditions he had missed out on, burnt food or not. Thankfully, Tracy had agreed to spend Christmas Eve at his grandmother's house. He could already smell the glazed ham and hot chocolate; could hear Bing Crosby's velvety voice lined with a soft crackle from their record player. Always a real thirty-three LP, same one since his childhood. Speaking of—

"Do you want me to pick up a tree tomorrow, or is Dad doing that? For Grandma, I mean."

"For Grandma . . ." she repeated in a pondering tone. "Um, well. That's something we haven't had a chance to discuss with you, since you've been gone."

"I don't understand."

A pause fell over the line.

"Mom?"

"Why don't you come over tomorrow and your father can explain."

"Explain what?"

Muffled, she spoke to someone off the handset, then returned. "Sorry, I've gotta help clean up. We'll see you tomorrow, all right?"

Reece's jaw tightened. He was about to demand she fill him in but recalled her stressful evening. Relenting, he simply said good night. After all, if it was anything critical, his mother would have told him.

Wouldn't she?

Chapter 3

Jenna steered through the heavy fog, pulse quickening. Her smearing wipers only worsened the view. Experimenting with the headlights didn't help. Six in the morning, but not a hint of light, save for the blinding beams from passing commuters.

She reduced her speed, eyes trained on the solid white line running parallel to the guardrail. In the tree-laden hills overlooking Portland, the Skyline neighborhood was considered one of the most affluent, but come January, their snaking boulevard would turn slick enough for a luge.

It took a little patting to find the defrost button by feel. The second she turned it on she realized her grave mistake. Warm air flooded the windshield and thickened the haze. Resisting panic, she scrambled for the knob to shut it off. In the process she hit the radio button, launching "Carol of the Bells" through the airwaves.

Deeeng . . . donnng . . . deeeeng . . . donnng . . .

The monotonous loop intensified as she rolled down the window. She poked her head out to see the road, braving the blast of cold.

Deeeng . . . donnng . . . deeeeng . . . donnng . . .

What the heck was she doing, risking her life to save a measly shoebox? Trading in her nice sedan for this two-door tin can should have reinforced her need to say no. Her first mistake had been to let her old boyfriend talk her into buying a condo together. "A good investment," he'd called it. Of course, she hadn't counted on him losing his job, or the realty bubble bursting. And when they split up, she didn't have much of a choice but to purchase his half.

This, she reminded herself, was the greatest reason for her drive through the misty blackness, her nose threatened by frostbite. Because there just might be a gem in that box Terrence found. He'd mentioned a container inside that appeared to hold jewelry. Clients often didn't realize what they owned. Like exploring a sunken ship, she needed only look under the right plank. A single treasure could seal the deal with her boss: "You get me a fifteen percent increase over the last estate, and I'll make you a partner." That's what he'd agreed to after months of Jenna's requests, all posed as a win-win; her boss could focus on other ventures, and Jenna, his top employee, would earn them even more if she was personally invested. Her goal finally had clarity, same as the view now through the windshield.

She pulled her head back inside. Teeth chattering, she closed the window and silenced the radio in the midst of "Santa Baby." The lyrics were but a wish list of materialism, further support that the holiday came once a year too often. Two turns and a sharp curve later, Jenna parked at the base of the sloped driveway. Its steepness, she'd been told, was part of the rationale behind selling. With Mrs. Porter now living in her son's family home, her large Victorian house loomed dark and still.

At the curb stood a pile of half a dozen fully stuffed trash bags. Her crew would be filling many more of those before they were done. The thought made her happy; the idea of scrounging through them made her cringe.

She would check inside the home first.

The keys on her loop were labeled by house number, organized numerically. A good system in daylight. Prior to dawn, not so much. Judging by the keys' shapes, she went with her first guess. No luck. A second one glided easily into the lock but wouldn't turn. When she tried to slide it out, the key's metal teeth clenched and held, refusing to budge.

A squeak of brakes spun her around. A van rolled past. She still had time before the trash pickup. But how much?

Just then, the front door flew open. Her keys broke free and dropped to the ground. Fear of an intruder stalled her heart.

Then the silhouette gained definition, and Jenna recognized the person she had met briefly in passing.

"Mrs. Porter," she said with a sigh. "I didn't think you'd be here. I hope I didn't wake you."

"Of course not. I was up doing my Pilates."

At her age? She had to be in her late eighties, and wearing a pink frilly bathrobe, a scarf around her curlers.

"Wow, that's amazing. Really?"

The woman peered over her cat-eye glasses. "No, dear."

At first taken aback, Jenna smiled.

"Well, I suspect you're here to work. So have at it." Mrs. Porter shuffled toward the kitchen, flipping lights on as she went. Word had it, as the widow of a local college president, she was rarely seen in anything but her Sunday best. Predawn clearly afforded an exception.

"I'll be right here in the den," Jenna called out.

Mrs. Porter didn't respond.

Jenna shut the front door and hurried into the study. She yanked the chain of a desk lamp, illuminating the ceiling-high bookshelves. A layer of dust further aged the antique book collection. The room's paisley trim, burgundy curtains, and leather wingbacks were straight out of *Masterpiece Theatre*—but surrounded by junk.

When Jenna started a week ago, the stacks of decades-old magazines had been the first to go. Paper grocery bags and used gift wrap, even saved aluminum squares, had filled two whole recycle bins. Typical of Great Depression survivors, the woman "didn't like to waste."

Jenna's mother used to lean on the phrase when her so-called collecting began. She had never gotten as bad as those hoarders on TV; reality programs preyed on extremes. There had been no mold covering her floors. No cause for asthma or scabies. Although maybe, if the woman had continued denying help, that ultimately would have been her. She had certainly accumulated enough for Jenna to keep visitors away. Box after box of unopened items. Many purchases identical. The problem had grown steadily, ignited by Jenna's father. Specifically the day he ran off with a young coworker. As a salesman who'd traveled most of his daughter's life, he rarely reached out afterward. So the morning he called with news, Jenna had steeled herself: He was getting remarried. What she hadn't prepared for was the full impact that hit on Christmas Day, when the presents her mother had bought formed a blockade of half the tree.

Shoving down the memory, Jenna focused on the only boxes that mattered: the moving boxes in Mrs. Porter's study. One after the other she peeked beneath the unsealed flaps.

"Terrence, where'd you put it?" she muttered. She would hate to call him this early in the morning.

A packing popcorn crunched beneath her sneaker. She reached down to pick it up and noticed a shoebox on the floor nearby. She lifted the lid. A small handful of black-and-white snapshots lay in disarray. In the top one, a mix of male and female soldiers posed in a group. Their smiles shone bright, yet their faces appeared as worn as their khaki uniforms. Palm trees framed the backdrop of a pole tent marked with a thick red cross. It was a hospital, based somewhere tropical. World War II, Jenna would guess, though she knew little about the era beyond a few episodes of *Band of Brothers*.

She continued to rummage and retrieved a hardback copy of *Jane Eyre*. Worn edges, not an early edition. Nothing worth a price tag. Beneath the book was a velvety, hinged container. The last thing in the shoebox, it spurred a flicker of hope. She imagined a diamond bracelet tucked neatly inside. Ten carats. Perfectly cut. Rather, she discovered a Bronze Star.

"Damn."

Sure, plenty of buyers would pay a nice penny for this, re-enactors in particular. And technically the piece was fair game, since Mrs. Porter hadn't removed it from inventory. Regardless, not even Jenna could discount the importance it would hold for any client.

She took the shoebox down the hall, toward the whistle of a kettle. By the time she reached the kitchen, the steam was screaming at full volume.

"Excuse me. Mrs. Porter?"

The woman was on a step stool in her slippers. Her pale skin curved gently over thin cheeks. She opened one cupboard, then the next.

"Mrs. Porter," Jenna boomed, to no avail. Was she hard of hearing?

The kettle refused to relent.

"Here, I'll get that for you!" Jenna removed it from the stove and clicked off the burner.

The woman kept on searching.

Maintaining her volume, Jenna asked, "Could I help you with something?"

"You could stop hollering, for one. Gracious, I'm standing right here."

"Sorry, I thought . . ."

"My teapot."

"Pardon?"

Again, Mrs. Porter looked over the glasses perched on the tip of her narrow nose. "I would like to use my little Chinese teapot."

Jenna knew the item immediately. She'd found it in a hodge-podge of tea sets they would soon be displaying for sale. "My friend Sally has that one." At Mrs. Porter's furrowed brow, she explained, "She's a broker of collectibles, so she's helping appraise some things."

Jenna prided herself on her own assessment skills. However, a unique stamp on the base of the pot, suggesting the possibility of a higher price, called for a second opinion. "I assure you, she'll take very good care of it."

Mrs. Porter took this in, her frown slackening.

This was exactly the reason Jenna hated it when a client remained in the house. How do you handle a person's things—dumping worthless mementos, price tagging furnishings—while the owner hovered in the next room? Chattiness, too, never increased efficiency: *My goodness, was that in there? Where did you find that? Oh, you have to hear the funniest story about the day we bought that.*

Hopefully, Mrs. Porter didn't plan to stay long.

"So, I was wondering . . ." Jenna hid her earnestness. "Since I really hate to be in your way, do you happen to know when you'll be going back to your family's?"

Mrs. Porter snagged a ceramic mug and inspected it for cleanliness. "Not anytime soon from the looks of things."

"I . . . don't understand."

"The bedroom they stuck me in, down in the basement, it flooded in the middle of the night." She descended onto the linoleum. "While they're replacing the carpet, I'm not about to stay in a Holiday Inn when my real home is right here. For the time being, at any rate."

Repairs during the holidays were bad news—for all of them. Mrs. Porter jerked her chin upward. "What have you got there, dear?"

Jenna suddenly remembered the shoebox tucked against her hip. If the two of them were going to be sharing space for a while, winning the woman over would be wiser than making her an enemy.

Smile in place, Jenna set the box on the nearest counter. "Terrence stumbled across these when he was sorting. We figured you'd like to save them."

Mrs. Porter put down her cup, a question on her face. She raised the lid and picked up a photo. Within seconds, her squinting turned wide-eyed. A small gasp slipped from her wrinkled lips. As her fingertips traced the picture, an invisible shell seemed to melt from her body. Her eyes, brown as bark, turned moist and soft with memories.

Jenna couldn't resist a closer look. A serviceman was holding a tiny branch, in the manner of mistletoe, over the nurse's head. His gaze was a combination of mischief and adoration, and despite the snapshot's lack of color, the young woman appeared to be blushing.

"Is this you?" Jenna asked softly. "Is that how you and your husband met, during the war?"

Mrs. Porter's eyes snapped up. Hand shaking, she dropped the picture. Jenna swiftly reached down for the keepsake, but when she attempted to give it back, Mrs. Porter went steely and cool.

"I'm so sorry," Jenna said. "I didn't mean to upset you."

"Throw them away."

Jenna stared. Mrs. Porter couldn't possibly mean that. She was just rattled from her recollections. No question, the woman would regret the decision later, when it was too late to reverse.

"You know what," Jenna reasoned, "why don't I set these

aside somewhere. I'm sure once you've had a chance to think it over—"

Mrs. Porter broke in loud and firm. "Toss them out, donate them, do as you'd like. But take . . . them . . . away."

Jenna hesitated, still stunned, before returning the picture to the pile. Stoically, Mrs. Porter turned and left the kitchen. A history unspoken trailed her like crumbs.

Chapter 4

"I can't believe you're selling her house," Reece spat the moment he entered the garage.

At the greeting, his father slid out from under the antique Ford truck. Dabs of oil tinted his thin charcoal hair and an old T-shirt that outlined his slight paunch. His initial look of surprise hardened as Reece's words set in. He gave his hands a strong wipe with a soiled rag as he rose to his full height of six-two, evening their gazes.

"I take it your mother filled you in."

"She told me enough."

"Then you ought to understand why having your grandma here makes sense. Imagine if I hadn't been there when she tripped and—"

"And she's fine."

"This time, yes," his father pointed out. "But it just proved what I've been saying. She needs people around to help her."

"So hire somebody."

"It's more than that. I told you before, the place is too big to take care of by herself."

"Fine. Then get her a housekeeper."

The man huffed a laugh that clawed at Reece's nerves. It was the same reaction from years ago when Reece asked him to cosign for his first car. And when he asked for help with his college tuition. Looking back, Reece's decision to drop out might even have been retaliation for that laugh.

His dad hadn't found the choice quite as amusing.

Frustrating thing was, as a longtime security officer for a prestigious bank, his frugal father always had plenty of funds put away. Eventually, Reece had learned not to ask for a single thing. But this was different.

This wasn't about him.

Done with the conversation, his father ducked beneath the Ford's open hood and adjusted plugs on the motor. The expensive toy rarely left the garage. He kept it stored away for fear of the tiniest scratch. Now he wanted to do the same to his own mother.

Over time, since her husband's death, Grandma Estelle's activities of quilting groups and bridge clubs had lessened to none. But she did keep up with her garden and "puttering" in her house. Take those away, and the grandma he adored might fade as well.

"If she doesn't want to move," Reece contended, "she shouldn't have to."

His father responded with a mumble, clearly half listening. Reece decided to say something that would make more of an impact.

"Just because you want to cash in on the sale doesn't mean you have the right to force her out of her own house." That one worked. His father drew his head back and stood with a glower, tinged with confusion. "Your grandpa left that house to me for a reason. He trusted I'd make sure she was taken care of."

"Yeah," Reece said, "I'm sure staying in my old, flooded

bedroom was exactly what Grandpa had in mind." With that, he turned to leave.

He was about to step outside when his father yelled, "Reece!" The tone carried a deep gruffness so seldom used Reece couldn't help but stop. He wheeled back around as his father stepped closer, hands hitched on his hips. "You wanna tell me what the hell this is really about?"

Not until asked the question did Reece realize the core of the issue, at least between them. Never off duty, the guy was always sizing Reece up, judging him. Policing his acts like a dictator of safety. After the snowmobile crash, Reece had felt enough guilt at the hospital without his father charging in, shouting, "With all the crazy stunts you pull, how many times have I warned you something like this would happen?"

Reece considered explaining this now. Yet there was no point giving his father the satisfaction of knowing it still bothered him. Besides, what would come of it? His dad was far from the type to acknowledge his own faults.

In the silence, the man took a calming breath through his nose. "Look, son, I don't know what's eating at you. But after talking it through, even your grandmother agreed it was the right decision." At Reece's lack of response, his dad headed back to the engine. "You don't believe me, you go ask her yourself."

An unnecessary suggestion. That's precisely what Reece planned to do.

Along the curb lined with typical suburban homes, Jenna sat calculating. If she hurried in and out, she'd have plenty of time to grab lunch somewhere before meeting Sally about the appraisals. Fortunately, the collectibles broker, with a work ethic rivaling Jenna's, didn't balk at an appointment on Thanksgiving weekend. Otherwise, today would have been chalked up as largely unproductive on Jenna's list.

Cataloging and adding to inventory sheets had been a challenge after her encounter with Mrs. Porter. Unable to concentrate, Jenna had called it a day but followed orders by ridding the house of the shoebox. She could think of three collectors off the top of her head who loved buying World War II memorabilia. For the time being, though, the box would wait in her trunk. Based on the emotion she had witnessed, she'd be surprised if Mrs. Porter didn't have second thoughts.

As Jenna stepped out of the car, a rumble caught her ear. Across the street, a driver was struggling to start an SUV. Reflections of gray clouds shaded the windshield. The possibility of offering to help zipped through Jenna's mind. Then again, thanks to modern communication, who today wasn't fully capable of handling a little car trouble?

She continued toward the Tudor-style house of Mrs. Porter's son and his wife, Sandy. The woman had promised Jenna a key to an upstairs storage closet at the Porter estate. Hopefully, like all the other closets in the home, there would be items of decent monetary value that just needed a dusting or polish. Perhaps while here she could also determine how long before the elderly woman could return to her new residence.

Jenna had almost made it to the driveway when the slam of a car door turned her head. The driver leaned back against the SUV and raked his fingers through his dark brown hair, inadvertently causing his bangs to spike. He blew out a breath that said it was one of those days.

Jenna urged herself to stick with her plan, but something about his expression—a frustration that ran deep and familiar—wouldn't let go. She peeked at her watch. With a grumble, she decided she could always eat *after* the meeting, if needed.

Approaching the guy, she became acutely aware of his athletic build, outlined by a navy polo shirt tucked into belted slacks.

More intriguing than that, from his profile, she noticed a pink dot on his earlobe from a hole that had been allowed to close. Something about the story there made her smile.

"Is there some way I can help?"

He raised his head with a start. The instant their eyes connected, a fluttering arose in Jenna's chest. He held her gaze for a long moment, or maybe it only seemed that way, until he replied, "The battery. I think it's done for good."

"Do you need to borrow a phone?" she managed.

"I called Triple A already. Guess I was willing to give it one last shot."

Jenna could relate; she started her own vehicle every morning with the same attitude. Suddenly, she remembered the cables in the hidden compartment of her trunk. "Do you want me to jump you?"

When he went to speak but paused, she reviewed her question. "I meant, in your car." Oh, jeez. That sounded worse. "Not *in*," she corrected, "*on.*"

What was she saying? A burn filled her cheeks.

"I mean I can grab jumper cables—if you'd like."

Any trace of earlier angst in his face dissolved. His lips curved into a smile that he appeared to be stifling. "I'd love that."

Jenna cringed inside. Since when did any guy, let alone a stranger, make her so flustered? Her sole salvation was the subtle blush tinting his olive-toned cheeks.

"I'll drive over."

She moved her car to face the SUV before retrieving her cables. Behind the shield of her raised trunk, she exhaled. Thankfully her nerves settled as she and the driver focused on their tasks. Popping hoods, connecting batteries, revving motors. She did her best to detour from his gaze. After the mess left from her last boyfriend, she didn't need another complication.

Life was better without the clutter.

Done helping, she leaned into her trunk to put the cables

away. When she turned around, the guy was standing behind her. The view of her backside in faded jeans topped with an old sweatshirt couldn't have been all that appealing.

Not that she wanted it to be.

She closed the trunk. "So, you're all set."

"I really appreciate your help—" He stopped and shook his head. "I didn't even ask your name."

"It's Jenna." She stuck out her hand in reflex and immediately wished she hadn't. The touch of his hand only resurrected those damn flutters.

"Well, Jenna, I can't tell you how grateful I am."

"It was nothing. Really."

In the midst of their lingering shake, warm as the deep tone of his voice, Jenna's stomach groaned. Gratefully. A reminder of lunch, and her meeting. She withdrew her hand. "I'd better get going or I'll be late."

The corners of his eyes crinkled with lines of regret. "I'm sorry to keep you," he said, and added, "Take care."

"You too." She hastened off to snag her keys and purse from her car, but then chose to wait in her seat until he drove away, avoiding another exchange.

Once in the clear, she hazarded a look at the dashboard clock. If she left this very minute, she could make it on time. But that would mean having to swing by here again later.

Though aggravated, she dashed outside and up the driveway.

Her second ring of the doorbell succeeded in summoning Sandy Porter, who was busy listening to someone on a cordless phone. She ushered Jenna inside and motioned her hand like a bird's beak to indicate the caller was a chatterbox.

"I agree," Sandy said into the mouthpiece. "I definitely think you should bring that up at the next committee meeting." Charitable boards and events appeared to fill her schedule. All were likely important enough, but Jenna didn't have time today for patience.

"The key," Jenna whispered, using her own hand motion to illustrate.

Sandy vigorously nodded, bouncing her twisted-up do. Her nails and lips were glossed in pink, perfect matches to her sweater set. Continuing their game of charades, she raised her pointer finger—*Be back in one minute*—and ambled off around the corner.

Jenna flicked at the side seam of her jeans, an anxious countdown. She could hear Sandy rustling through a drawer and commenting cheerily on the phone.

That's when Jenna glimpsed an image in the formal room. On the white fireplace mantel stood a framed photo of the SUV's driver, drawing her across the span of cream carpet. Was he part of the family?

She picked up the picture to take a better look. A vast waterfall behind him, a backpack on his shoulder, he beamed with a ruggedness that glimmered in his eyes. He was attractive, sure, and had loads of charm. But there was something more.

"Oh, here you are!" Sandy entered the room. "Sorry about the phone. Auction season. The thing rings off the hook."

Jenna fumbled with the frame to prop it back in place. "No problem. I was just . . . wiping a smudge." She pushed up a smile. "Occupational habit."

Sandy tilted her head at the photo with a prideful glow. "That's our son at Multnomah Falls. Reece and his sister, Lisa, used to go hiking there every summer, before she moved to Washington. You just missed them both, actually."

Jenna strained to absorb anything that followed his name. *Reece.* She switched to the first topic that came to mind. "By the way, I had a question about . . . Mrs. Porter."

"Go on, shoot." Sandy smiled.

You're a salesperson, Jenna told herself. *Spin this.*

"The thing is, I have some items of hers that seemed pretty

important. A box of old pictures from when Mr. and Mrs. Porter served in the military. Even a Bronze Star from World War Two. But when I asked her, she told me to toss it all out."

Sandy didn't ponder this for more than a second. "It couldn't have been them. Probably just some people they knew."

"But the woman in the photos—her features looked so similar."

"Hmm . . . maybe a cousin, then. I couldn't tell you. But I do know Bill's father never enlisted. Because of flatfoot, I think. And goodness knows, Estelle isn't the type to have enlisted in the *military*." Sandy laughed softly.

When it came to personal items, Jenna welcomed the invitation to do as she pleased. She just wished she could as easily discard Mrs. Porter's reaction.

"So you *don't* think they're worth saving?" Jenna wanted final confirmation.

"From what Estelle told you, doesn't sound like it. Besides, even though she has a great little setup here, with a kitchenette and its own compact washer and dryer, I'm afraid there isn't a lot of storage space."

Jenna nodded. The subject was settled.

"Anyhow, this is for you," Sandy said.

The key. Jenna had nearly forgotten. She accepted the offering, which brought back her other concern: How long until the flooded bedroom was repaired?

Before Jenna could ask, a phone rang in the kitchen.

"Ooh, I need to catch that," Sandy said, stepping away. "Would you mind letting yourself out, sweetie?"

"Um—no. That's fine."

"Thanks a bunch!" Sandy waved and disappeared into the next room.

Releasing a sigh, Jenna headed out.

After sending a text—**On my way!**—she drove toward her

meeting. Houses on every block were in the midst of being Christmas-ized. Neighbors were hanging prickly wreaths, untangling knotted lights. Planting huge plastic candy canes in perfectly good lawns.

Today, though, Jenna was barely irritated over the scene. Despite her better judgment, her thoughts kept channeling back to the mystery of Estelle Porter's past.

Chapter 5

The system had become a clustered mess. Thousands of international shipments continued to arrive at stores with no clear tracking of details. For Reece, this meant an emergency campout at the office, regardless of it being Thanksgiving weekend. Even if the holiday were observed by his biggest London account, it wouldn't matter. Reece and his IT team were ordered to fix the problem before Europe's retailers opened for morning business.

For yet another hour Reece left his techies to their mission. In his office he'd tried calling his grandma, but her house phone had been disconnected. His father hadn't wasted any time. If there was any chance of making it over before she went to bed, he needed the Brit issue solved.

"Making any progress?" he said, peeking into IT's cubical area.

One of them mumbled "sorta" and the three continued typing away. They slouched before their computers with four screens each. Why the hell they needed as many screens as the CIA was beyond Reece, but now wasn't the time to raise the question.

He glanced inside the pizza box on the closest desk and found a lone slice. The six-pack of Mountain Dew he'd brought in, bribery for the two caffeine addicts of the bunch, was nearly gone. He wished he could think of something else to speed up the group.

"Anything more I can get you guys?"

Instead of responding, over their shoulders the three exchanged codes and technical speak to facilitate their test cases. The mood was sluggish and gray. But then, he couldn't blame them for not being enthused. Working today hadn't been part of Reece's plan either.

After getting his car battery replaced that morning, he had zoomed onto the freeway, headed for his grandma's house. Thoughts of Jenna, the stunning woman he'd just met, had disengaged his auto-pilot skills. When his cell phone rang, he realized he'd missed the turnoff—by three full exits. His boss's call about the integration disaster had rooted him back in reality.

"I tried to tell them," Reece had insisted, "rushing the SAP cut-over was a bad idea." Ignoring his warning, some hotshot exec had demanded they implement the complicated system right before a global launch of a winter clothing line. A real genius.

"I know, I know," his boss had said. "But unless we want to lose millions, you'd better round up your guys right away."

Reece had groaned his compliance. In the background, he could hear people talking and laughing, band music blasting from a televised football game.

"Bet you wish you'd taken me up on my invite, huh?" A smirk in the man's tone.

"Hell yeah," Reece had replied, though hadn't actually meant it. Even with the two feet of fresh snow on Mount Hood, rarely seen this early in the year, a snowboarding trip had lost its appeal.

He now grabbed the last slice of pepperoni pizza and called out to his team, "I'll be down the hall if you need me." An ugly mountain of nonurgent e-mails had piled up during his travels. At least that would keep him busy until receiving his cue to help put out the logistical fire.

Reece journeyed through the ghost town of a floor to reach his office. He took a bite of his cooled pizza and plopped down in his chair. On the corner of his desk was a digital frame he'd grown so accustomed to that he barely noticed its auto slide show anymore. He had forgotten this particular picture, of him and Tracy in a stall beside her horse. He'd never been much of an animal person, yet he'd volunteered to groom Chestnut until Tracy was well enough to do it herself. The horse gradually grew on him.

Reece smiled at the memory of the first time Chestnut nuzzled his neck, a sign of affection and acceptance, of trust. That was the day Tracy snapped the photo.

The picture faded from the screen, replaced by a shot of the Graniellos. Or "Granolas," as Tracy called them.

"A bunch of fruits and nuts," she liked to joke, "all packed into one big family."

He laughed to himself now, before a realization struck: Tracy was the one he should have been thinking about all morning, not some stranger who'd helped him with his car. And yet somehow, he couldn't shake the buzzing thrill he'd felt while near Jenna, from touching her hand. The raw beauty she projected.

He stopped there, scrapped the wandering thought. "Now who's the genius?" he muttered, and threw his pizza away.

Cold feet. That's all this was. Natural nerves about taking the next step.

He'd learned the hard way not to follow emotions over logic. Snowmobiling at Mount Hood had taught him that. With Tracy on the backseat, they'd been cruising along, having a great time, when adrenaline lured him into an impromptu race with a guy on the next snowmobile.

"Reece, you're going too fast," he'd vaguely heard her say. Wind and snowflakes blew at his ears, at the mask over his eyes. Tracy clung to his middle as they approached a curve. If he cut the corner around a tree, no doubt they'd take the lead.

"Slow down!" Maybe her words had come too late. Maybe he'd ignored them, driven by the need to win a no-win contest. There had been no judges. No finish line. Just the rush of hitting a snow-covered rock that launched them into the air, a slow motion flight, rewarding him with a broken arm—and the scare of his life at seeing Tracy's limp form at the base of a tree.

"Oh, dear God, please . . ." he begged, after crawling over to her. "Please be all right."

Her cloudy breaths kept him from breaking down until they reached the hospital, where a doctor diagnosed her fractured pelvis.

"My horse," she'd said groggily once she was told the news.

At her bedside, Reece gingerly squeezed her hand. "I'll take care of him, don't worry," he told her. "And I swear, Tracy, I'll never do anything that hurts you again."

Out of fear now of breaking that promise, something inside him was looking for a way out. That had to be it. That's where all these doubts were coming from. Any fascination with another woman had no place in his life. The time had come to take the leap, to ask the big, looming, inevitable question.

But to do that properly, there was one thing Reece needed: a special heirloom with a history he hoped to repeat.

Chapter 6

Jenna sat up on her white leather couch, reading it once again. Ad copy for the estate sale shouldn't have been this difficult to proof. Terrence had penned a nice write-up, as he always did. Wisely, this time he mentioned the family's name. Mr. Porter's former status as the president of a local college could attract more buyers. Even small-celebrity interest helped.

She leafed through her folder, moving on to her task sheet. The meeting with Sally hadn't gone as she'd hoped, most of the items not appraising for more than Jenna guessed. "Let me keep checking on these," Sally had told her, regarding the last two uncertainties.

A slow economy wasn't helping Jenna's cause. The fifteen percent increase she'd promised, and thus her partnership, were slipping from her grasp. Squashing the prospect, she racked her brain for any collectors she'd forgotten to contact. Not a single one emerged. Granted, her resources weren't the problem. It was her thoughts, which kept floating back to a vision of Estelle. And the woman's shoebox. And her grandson.

Business and pleasure don't mix, she reminded herself, citing her boss's basic rule. A clichéd concept but valid nonetheless. In fact, it was one her father had bulldozed right through, leaving Jenna and her mother in his trampled wake.

She shut the file, tossed it aside, and snagged the remote. Reclining, she flew from one channel to the next. A cheesy talk show, a political debate, a slew of reality shows. She kept flipping until she landed on a movie featuring stars she recognized. Cuba Gooding Jr. and Ben Affleck—in *Pearl Harbor*.

The connection to Estelle screamed as loud as the bombs dropping onto the navy ships before her.

Jenna resumed her channel surfing. Eventually she stopped on an infomercial. She treated TV ads and pawning programs like a game, challenging herself to guess the price. Make that two prices: first, the product's worth; second, what it would sell for. She was seldom off by much.

In this one, a bearded man demonstrated a cabinet with a zillion compartments. All silver and glass, it matched everything in Jenna's perfectly sparse condo.

The infomercial broke for a commercial—a great irony in that. Black-and-white footage of Nat King Cole filled the screen. He crooned "For Sentimental Reasons" into an oversized microphone. As song titles scrolled upward, the shot changed to another man singing "I'm in the Mood for Love." It was a CD collection of nostalgic songs, ballads from the 1940s.

The war years.

Jenna arched a brow. "You've gotta be kidding me."

She shut the TV off.

From the beginning, Jenna had made a habit of giving clients their space. Anything unrelated to their houses and furnishings was their own business. For her, it was all about the sale. But . . . never before had she felt stalked by a person's history. By the likes of a shoebox, stored in her car trunk. Something in it kept prodding.

If only she could identify the source, like locating a pebble in her shoe, she could shake the problem away. Not with an intrusive investigation, just a quick online search. A few public records. Available to anyone.

Before she could change her mind, she dragged her soft briefcase closer and pulled out her laptop. As it warmed up, the rumble of a passing truck rose from three floors below. The motion rattled her large windows. She typed the keywords: *Estelle Porter Oregon.*

An obituary for the woman's husband, Walter, gave a brief summary of his life. No military service, which aligned with Sandy's claim. It mentioned his surviving widow, Estelle Agnes Martin. Besides her maiden name, there was nothing of note.

Jenna skimmed through several other entries, using the name Martin as well. But most of the links pertained to a beer company, specializing in porters, and some PTA president in Oregon, Wisconsin. No info about the right Estelle.

Probably a good thing.

Jenna tried to end the search, yet couldn't. She despised giving up on anything so easily. She stared at the blinking cursor, considering options, and tried: *Estelle Martin military WWII Pacific.*

The page refreshed with all new listings. It took Jenna a mere second to see that the fifth one down contained every one of the keywords. Anticipation flowed through her as she clicked on the link and discovered a site honoring members of the Women's Army Corps, called WACs, of World War II. She picked up speed, reviewing the pages, searching for Estelle's name.

At last, in an album of photographs, she found it in a caption:

(From left to right) *Pvt. Betty Cordell, Pvt. Shirley Davidson, PFC Rosalyn "Roz" Taylor, and Pvt. Estelle Martin.*

The corresponding picture appeared to feature the very faces from those in Estelle Porter's box. So why would she have hidden the achievement from her family? At least that's what she seemed to be doing, based on Sandy's comments.

Jenna scanned the next few pages in search of an answer, and froze. Not at the photo in particular but its caption. For below the image of Estelle with a handsome soldier, the same one who'd fashioned mistletoe from a branch, was the man's name: *Corporal Tom Redding*.

In other words, he wasn't the late Mr. Porter.

Ideas whirled. Perhaps the corporal was an old flame who'd never made it home. It would make sense, why Estelle didn't want the box. Especially if no one in the family knew of him. Better to rid yourself of objects that tethered you to the past. Jenna understood that firsthand. Plus, given the sparkle in the man's eyes, the glow in his smile, he would clearly take effort to forget.

In fact, he radiated the same type of charm as Estelle's grandson. There couldn't be a connection—could there?

"Oh, stop it."

She closed down her computer and set off for bed. Whether possible or not, such theories were none of her concern.

Chapter 7

"You don't have to do this," Reece insisted.

"What, keep meat on your bones?" his grandma said. "You sure you want to leave that to your mother?" She smirked from her stove, dressed in a pastel yellow sweater and gray woolen pants. Early-afternoon light angled through the window, creating a silvery outline of her soft curls.

Parked in a kitchen chair, Reece folded his arms. "Grandma, you know what I'm talking about."

More stirring of the chowder. More evading his question.

She scooped a ladleful into a bowl. The aroma of comfort food filled the room, just as it had for as long as Reece could remember. He couldn't count how many PB&J sandwiches or bowls of goulash he'd enjoyed at this very table. No one in history could top Grandma Estelle's zucchini bread or strawberry jam, both made of produce grown in her own backyard.

Reece cringed at the idea of a stranger moving in, tromping through that very garden. He tried to keep the frustration from his tone. "Regardless of what the paperwork says, this is your home. Dad has no right to make you move if you want to stay."

"Well, he hasn't called in a SWAT team quite yet," she said, delivering his soup and spoon. Per her usual, she would eat only after everyone else was taken care of. "Eat up, now, before you shrivel away."

"Grandma, please. I'm being serious."

She lowered herself into the chair across from him and stifled a cough. With a tissue plucked from her pocket, she dabbed at her nose. Her tired eyes surveyed the room, giving away what she wouldn't verbalize. No doubt, the wooden shelves of Goebel figurines and decorative plates and Amish carvings carried visions of her and her husband purchasing them together. Items that would soon be hawked off to a herd of bargain seekers.

Her gaze settled back on Reece. "Change is rarely easy, dear. Sometimes we just do what needs to be done."

"You know that's not a real answer."

She gestured to his bowl. "At least take a sip, or I'll start feeling insulted."

Given her spunk, a person might take her for the type to speak her piece without pause. Indeed this applied to day-to-day minutiae; though ironically, when it came to the most affecting decisions, she remained a traditional housewife and mother who dutifully complied. It would take more nudging—but not badgering—to uncover what she really wanted.

For now, he blew on a spoonful of soup and swallowed it down. His chest warmed from the hearty, perfectly salted chowder. He wondered how often she cooked for others these days, or did anything social that she used to love.

"Have you seen any of your old friends lately?"

"Which ones?" She dabbed at her nose again. "They're all old."

"I don't know. The ones you used to make quilts with."

"Now, why would I want to spend my Saturdays with blind old biddies, sticking myself with needles?"

"Well, when you put it that way . . ." Reece chuckled.

His grandma then veered to a safer realm, a basic catch-up on his life. Between sips he filled her in about work, and how his team had managed to salvage an account the day before. In the middle of his logistical recap, his thoughts looped back to the photo on his desk, reminding him of the second reason he'd come here today.

Still, unsure how to ask, he detoured to highlights of his recent travels. He described the weather, landscape, and culture in London and Seoul. "Did you and Grandpa ever visit Asia together?"

"We talked about taking a vacation there, but never got around to it."

Reece nodded, remembering how he and his sister used to gobble up popcorn while admiring the couple's travel photos, compliments of a white wall and a projector that tended to stick every ten slides.

At the silent lull, his grandmother tilted her head at him. "Dear, is there something else on your mind?"

He cleared the nerves from his throat, done stalling. "I was wondering if . . . well, you remember my girlfriend, Tracy?"

His grandma scrunched her brow.

Dumb question. As a longtime hospice volunteer, his grandmother had given him plenty of helpful tips about Tracy's daily care—sponge baths around her bandages, helping her out of bed.

"My point is, we've been dating for more than two years, and . . . she's amazing. Her family's great and . . ."

"And," his grandmother finished, "you're going to propose."

Embarrassed yet relieved she had said it for him, Reece explained, "You and Grandpa had such a great marriage. Guess I was hoping I could borrow your ring for good luck."

She gazed down at her vacant wedding finger, then rubbed at the loose skin that had prompted her to retire the ring into a jewelry box. "One thing I've learned, you don't need luck for a happy marriage. It's something you work at every day."

Reece didn't know how to respond. Maybe he should have waited. She was already losing so many belongings she valued. "If you'd prefer to keep it, I'd completely understand."

Ignoring the assurance, she continued, "But if you love this girl with all your heart"—a warm smile lifted her cheeks—"I know your grandpa would've been honored to pass it along."

Responsibility pressed onto his shoulders, as if his grandfather's hands were reaching down. Reece came around the table and gave her a hug, taking care not to squeeze too hard. "Thanks, Grandma."

"My pleasure, dear." She patted his back.

As he stood, she added, "I'll have your mother bring the ring here when she stops by tomorrow. Why don't you come over on Monday, and I'll have it shined up and ready for you?"

"That'd be wonderful."

Once they traded good-byes, he threw on his coat and scarf and headed for the front door. His grip was on the handle when he glanced into the formal room, where items were strewn across a long folding table, prepped to be priced.

Any other year, a fresh-cut tree would already be centered before the large picture window. Its decor never mimicked a store display, color coordinated and too pretty to touch. Instead, the ornaments were a hodgepodge of random shapes and handmade crafts, each holding a special memory . . . .

A noise from upstairs sliced through the thought. Reece strained to hear more. Over the years, thanks to the surrounding forest areas, he'd been credited with ridding the place of a bird, a mouse, and even a bat that had entered through the attic.

He grabbed a newspaper and rolled it up. At the top of the stairs, he waited, listening. Another sound seeped from the guest room on the right, the one he'd used for his overnight stays since childhood. He clutched his weapon and cautiously opened the door. The sight of a person caused him to jump.

With a gasp, the woman spun to face him. Then she released an audible breath, hand over her chest. "Goodness, Reece, you scared me."

His reflexive demand of *Who the hell are you?* died at the

recognition of his name. Wait . . . the girl he'd met yesterday. Outside his parents' house. "Jenna?"

She raised her hand in an awkward wave.

His delight from seeing her again whirled into a mix of surprise and utter confusion. "What are you doing here?"

"When I saw your car outside, I—I thought about coming back later to give you and your grandma privacy. But my crew's off till Monday, and I had some inventory to do, and—" She paused, slowing herself, and smiled. "Sorry if I disturbed you."

The pieces were assembling: the clipboard in her left hand, the moving boxes, the filled trash bags.

"You're the one selling off my family's things."

She opened her mouth, then closed it, as if thrown by his statement. Uncertainty washed over her features. "I've been assigned to this property, yes. But I assure you, we're a professional company."

Reece glimpsed his baseball, setting off an internal alarm. The ball rested on the inside lip of a white trash bag tipped onto the floor. He pulled it out, running his thumb over the seams, ratty from use. "You're throwing this away?"

She shook her head. "No."

He relaxed a fraction, before she added, "The white bags are for donations."

As in, doling them out for free? Dumping them at The Salvation Army?

"No way you're doing that. My grandfather caught this. It was the first Mariners game he ever took me to."

She straightened her posture and spoke evenly. "You're welcome to keep it if you'd like."

Thanks for your permission, he expressed through a huff. What else of value was she planning to toss out? Reece sifted through an open box on the bed and picked out a pennant flag from his UCLA years. His mother always cleared out memorabilia with every passing stage of his life. But his grandparents were different. His room here had been a precious time capsule.

Until now.

Jenna gripped her clipboard with both hands. "If the flag is special to you, please, take it. But my work here is under contract. Everything of significant sales value is considered frozen inventory."

"Inventory? This isn't a store."

"I'm sorry if this is hard for you," she offered. "But it's a job my company takes great pride in—"

"Yeah. The pride of a vulture."

Her lips flattened into hard lines before he registered the full harshness of his remark. Jenna, specifically, wasn't the villain here.

"Listen," he tried to explain, "this wouldn't be happening if it was up to me. There are things here that are really special."

"Yes," she bit out, "I know. *Everything* is special to *everyone.*" She stopped abruptly and lowered her gaze.

Reece sought appropriate words, all of which eluded him— as did the true root of his anger. All he knew was he wanted to halt time. Or, better yet, to go back to a period when life made sense. He glanced down at his hands, at the cracked letters of his pennant, his grandpa's weathered ball. Finally, at a loss, he dropped both items into the box and walked away.

Chapter 8

Jenna hurried through the entrance and scanned the chattering crowd. Decorative saddles and rodeo posters adorned the restaurant walls. She located her mother in a far booth; the profile of her bangs were tough to miss.

As Jenna threaded through the room, empty peanut shells cracked underfoot. The scent of barbecue ribs and the sizzling of steaks made her light-headed, or perhaps it was simply the good news. And good news was definitely what she needed after yesterday's run-in with Reece Porter. If she had known better from the start, she never would have helped the arrogant, self-righteous jerk.

The single upside of their last exchange was the amount of work she had plowed through after he'd left. Some people eat when they're upset, some exercise, others bake. Jenna organized. *Toss, repair, sell, sell. Toss, repair, sell, sell.*

Still, she'd been unable to fully purge her frustrations, most of which were at herself, for letting him get under her skin. It wasn't like Reece had said or done anything worse than a handful of other clients' emotionally charged relatives. Yet from him, the words and glares came with tentacles. They'd latched on and kept her reeling half the night. Pondering. Justifying. Far more people were grateful for her services, simplifying an overwhelming chore after a loved one's passing or when downsizing to a retirement home.

Fortunately, today's announcement had pried away Reece's hold.

"Sorry I'm late." Jenna scooted into the seat across from her mother. She plopped down her purse beside the mini-bucket of peanuts. "I was about to leave when I got some fun news."

"Did you get my message?" Her mom religiously phoned the day of their monthly luncheons to confirm their date.

"Oh, I forgot to check it," Jenna confessed. "I was on the other line with Sally—which is what I have to tell you about. Apparently, the director of the Portland History Museum was scheduled to be a guest on *Good Day Northwest*. You know, the morning show?" Reliving her earlier excitement, Jenna didn't wait for affirmation. "The woman was slated to promote a Jackie O exhibit. But since they're in-between curators, things slipped through and they didn't get proper clearance from the family trust. So now there's no new exhibit, and ... anyway ..." Back to the point.

"Since Sally's the one who helped arrange the TV spot through her producer friend, she was trying to help find another guest. And turns out, they liked the idea of me doing a segment about appraising used jewelry. As part of a budgetwise series for the holidays."

"Wow. That's fantastic." Her mother's eyes shone bright with anticipation, her makeup remarkably toned down. "But, honey, about my message ..."

"Gosh, sorry. I'm rambling." Jenna laughed at herself, wondering if she'd taken a single breath since arriving. "Why, what were you calling about?"

The conversation broke off as a man approached their table.

He was decked out in cowboy boots and a western shirt, like the rest of the themed staff, but with the added touch of a bolo tie. Maybe it denoted employee of the month.

"You must be Jenna," he said.

He knew her name? Oh, boy. Ten minutes late, and her mother had already loaded the waiter up with too many details. Jenna hoped it wasn't meant as a setup, since the guy had to be in his fifties.

She was about to ask for a minute to peek at the menu, when he slid into the booth beside her mother.

"Great to meet you finally." He offered Jenna his hand for a shake. "Your mother has raved on and on about you."

"Honey, this is Doobie," her mom chimed in. "The friend I've told you about. From the studio, remember?"

This was what Doobie looked like? A cowboy—in downtown Portland?

Her mother fidgeted with her fork. "*Jenna.*"

That's when it dawned on Jenna that she hadn't provided him with her hand in return. "Hi," she said, reaching out.

His palm was rough and his shoulders a bit thick, as if he'd been a football lineman back in the day. A crew cut appeared where Jenna had envisioned dreadlocks or a salt-and-pepper ponytail. Everything about his appearance surprised her— although nothing shocked her more than watching him now, draping an arm over her mom's shoulders. His blatant coziness eliminated any possibility of mere friendship.

"I hope you don't mind me joining you. Your mom and I were supposed to grab lunch tomorrow. But plans changed, and I need to meet my daughter, Ceci, for a gift exchange."

"I see." Jenna tried to say more, but her lips had gone numb.

"Besides, I told Rita, here, it's about time the two of us got introduced." He slanted a smile at Jenna's mom, making her giggle.

Jenna flashed back to her own reaction of first meeting

Reece. How foolish that now seemed. A passing attraction. No different than this, she assured herself. Since the divorce, her mother had occasionally mentioned dates that never developed into anything. Just because Doobie was the first to make Jenna's acquaintance didn't mean it was serious. After all, the guy already had his own family. No doubt that entailed enough emotional baggage to fill his whole pickup truck.

The thought sobered Jenna's mind. "So, you have kids."

"Just one daughter. About your age, actually."

"Were you married before?"

"Sure was."

"How long?"

"Oh, a smidge over ten years."

"What went wrong?"

Her mother snapped, "Jenna."

Maybe a business mode of appraising wasn't appropriate. Jenna hated to dull her mom's enthusiasm, just as she didn't enjoy informing clients that their perceived "treasure" was worth less than a latte. But in their best interest, someone had to be objective.

"It's okay, I don't mind." Doobie smiled. "When Ceci's mom started dating Gary—that's her husband now—I hear my daughter grilled him for hours." He laughed, visibly relaxing Jenna's mother, before he addressed the question.

"My ex and I were friends all through high school. Probably should've kept it that way. Good news is, we get along better nowadays than when we were married."

Jenna grappled with his answer. What was he saying? They might reunite as a couple one day? She was tempted to ask, but her mom intervened.

"Speaking of good news." Her segue came off forced and awkward, a direct reflection of this surprise meeting. "Jenna, tell him about the morning show."

The guest spot. A deflated topic.

None too soon, a waitress arrived with three mason jars of water. "Sorry for the wait, folks." She produced an order pad from the half apron over her jean skirt. "Are y'all ready?"

Jenna didn't know what she was ready for, only that she needed space to organize her thoughts. "You two go ahead and order."

Worry creased her mom's features. "Honey, you aren't leaving, are you?"

Doobie gently patted her mom's hand. The gesture, to Jenna, was equally sweet and terrifying. More reason to stick around.

"Of course not." She pasted on a smile. "I just need to hit the restroom."

The server moved aside as Jenna slid out.

Relief spread across her mom's face and lowered the shoulder pads of her sweater.

Jenna wove her way toward the bathroom, enticingly close to the exit. Again, shells crunched beneath her soles, the sounds like glass—like the memory of her youth, her mother—shattering.

This man could be the nicest guy on the planet, but if things didn't work out, what would happen to her mom? One more rejection, one wrong step, and *crack!* Would there be enough pieces to put back together?

Chapter 9

"Hello?" Reece hollered again from the base of the staircase.

No answer. No creaking on the floor above. Had he misremembered? He was sure his grandmother had said to stop by on his way to work, that her ring would be ready for him by then.

It's not as if he was on a deadline to propose. All the same, it was better not to lose momentum. "Grandma, are you home?"

She had to be around here somewhere. He strode through the dining room and on to the kitchen. Maybe she'd moved back into his parents' house already. But why leave the front door unlocked?

Oh, yeah—Monday. Jenna and her crew would be here soon. It was something he didn't like to think about. A call to his mom would confirm his grandma's whereabouts. With no working landline, he'd have to use his cell. Then he remembered: He'd left his mobile at home.

Great.

He turned for the hallway before he heard a voice, faint and strained. It came from the laundry room. A wisp of fear brushed

over the back of his neck. He rushed in and found his grandmother slouched on the floor in her bathrobe, leaned up against
the dryer. A load of damp laundry lay strewn across her lap.

He knelt beside her, his pulse pounding in his head. "What
happened? Are you all right?"

"It hurts . . . in my chest." Her breaths came sharp and
choppy. "My arm, I can't feel it."

A heart attack. Like his grandpa.

"I'll get some help. You're gonna be fine."

No phone. There was no phone to call. Damn his father.
And damn himself for forgetting his cell!

The hospital. It was less than ten minutes away.

"I've got you now." He fought the tremble in his tone as he
picked her up. One of her hands gripped his shirt. "I'm taking
you to the hospital."

Carrying her toward the entry, he kept a cautious pace, all the
while wanting to break into a run. He was nearly at his SUV
when two cars pulled up and parked along the curb. Jenna
Matthews jumped out and raced over in a panic.

"What happened?"

"She needs a doctor."

"Is there something I can do?"

He glanced into his passenger window. Work files and
empty water bottles littered the front seat. "Open the back
door," he told her, which she did in a blink.

"Here, I'll help you." Jenna hopped inside and guided
Mrs. Porter onto the backseat. "Go on and drive. I'll stay
with her."

Reece agreed and closed the door.

The instant he started the engine, he reversed out of the driveway, past Jenna's stunned coworkers. He shifted gears and
took off down the street.

"Slow down," he heard from the back. The same warning
Tracy had given on the mountain. This time he would heed it.

"That's it, just slow your breathing," Jenna soothed, and Reece realized she hadn't been talking to him. "There you go, Mrs. Porter, that's better."

In the rearview mirror he connected with Jenna's eyes. *Everything's going to be fine*, she seemed to tell him, her arm around his grandma's shoulders.

He hardly knew this person. Two days ago, he'd labeled her the enemy. Yet here she was, once more, coming to his rescue.

Back and forth, back and forth. Seated in the waiting area of the emergency room, Jenna watched Reece pace the tiled floor. He'd paused solely to phone his family, right after a nurse wheeled his grandmother off for examination.

"Why don't you sit down for a while," Jenna encouraged, as much for her own sake as his.

He stopped and glanced up at the wall clock. Relenting, he perched on the chair beside her. There were only two other people in the room, relatives of a man who had fallen from a ladder while stringing Christmas lights.

"I should've listened," Reece murmured.

Was that her cue to prod?

Eyes unseeing, he shook his head. "My dad said she needed someone around to watch her, but I wouldn't listen. And here I've been acting like a kid. How stupid is that? It's just a damn house."

Jenna thought of his baseball and pennant, displayed in a room he'd probably known since birth. All those objects tied to positive memories. "It's not stupid. That house is part of who you are." Her words were merely meant for assurance, but once out there, it dawned on her that she actually believed them.

Reece answered with a marginal nod, then began a nervous tapping on his knee. The sound turned the heads of the nearby couple, who already appeared to be on edge. Jenna gently touched Reece's hand to calm the movement. Although it worked, she hadn't planned on his fingers wrapping around hers. He looked at her with genuine warmth.

"Thanks for staying," he said.

Jenna had no real ties to Estelle Porter, yet here at Reece's side, she felt as though they were facing the crisis together.

Of course, in actuality they weren't. They were business acquaintances, which he too seemed to recall before he drew his hand away and broke from her gaze.

For several minutes they sat in the quiet, save for occasional noises from the hallway. The squeaking of shoes, the rolling of a hospital bed. In spite of her desire to stay, perhaps it was appropriate she leave.

As Jenna debated on how to slip out politely, a tall man in blue scrubs entered the room. Her chest tightened as he walked closer. Reece bristled in his seat, right before the doctor passed them to reach the visitors in the corner. The three spoke quietly, then left to see the patient.

Reece sank forward, elbows on his knees, intense with worry.

Jenna clasped her hands on her lap, resisting the urge to reach out again. "Your grandmother's a strong person. I'm sure she'll be fine."

He released a breath, resonant with doubt. "Ever since my grandpa died, she's needed someone to take care of her. I should've seen that and been around more."

At that moment, Jenna suspected he too had no idea of the woman's secret. A confession rose inside, fueled by a need to alleviate Reece's guilt. Or perhaps, more than that, to defend Estelle, a woman much too capable for pity.

"Did you know she was in the army?"

Lines formed on Reece's forehead. He stared as though she'd spoken in gibberish. "Who?"

"Your grandma. She served in World War Two. At some kind of field hospital." Right or wrong, Jenna's business or not, the truth was out there now.

"A hospital? She's never said anything."

"I found a box. Inside it was a Bronze Star and pictures of her in uniform, from serving in the Pacific."

"But . . . that can't be right," he said, processing. "The other day, she even told me, she's never been to that part of the world."

Jenna remembered the corporal in the photos, and a slew of deep-reaching theories returned. But that's all they were. Conjecture.

"I only brought it up so that you know she's a fighter. I imagine she's survived a lot worse."

Taking this in, Reece nodded slowly, then again with more surety. His eyes gained a mark of hope.

"Mr. Porter?" Another man in scrubs entered, spurring Reece to stand. Jenna also rose, praying Estelle's bravery had seen her through.

"Is my grandmother all right?"

The doctor's expression gave away nothing. "We've done an EKG and a chest X-ray. Both look good. We're just waiting on a few test results to rule everything out."

"What kind of tests? Are they also for her heart?"

"Some standard blood work. We want to be extra sure, but she appears to have simply suffered an inflammation of the lining of her lungs. Usually brought on by the flu, or even a common cold."

"So—not a heart attack?"

"That's right."

"But she was having problems breathing."

"From what I can tell," the doctor said, "it was just anxiety from what was happening. That's not uncommon." His mouth curved upward, a kind smile Jenna wished he had worn as he first approached. "At this point, she's being monitored. All her vitals are stable. We've given her a little something for the pain, so she's resting easy now. You can go in and visit her shortly."

Reece blew out a breath, a slight sheen in his eyes. "Thank you," he said, and the doctor departed. Relief washed over Jenna just as Reece swung around and embraced her. "God, I'm so glad she's okay."

"Me too," she said against his neck. Without warning, she found herself savoring the warmth of his skin and its faint earthy scent. The feel of his heart beating.

But then his grip loosened. He drew his head back and stared into her eyes. Mere inches separated their lips.

At the sound of voices in the hall, Reece stepped away. His parents had arrived. A glimpse at his father's face indicated he was questioning the scene. Given the situation, Jenna imagined how terrible this had to look. She edged backward, wishing she could disappear into the tan walls.

"Sweetie, is there any news yet?" Sandy asked Reece. Before he could relay the update, a nurse came to guide them. Sandy, noticing Jenna's presence, perked with surprise, then seemed to understand what had brought her here. She gave Jenna's arm a grateful squeeze on her way out, her husband leading the way.

Reece turned back with an awkward glance. "Thanks for your help."

"Sure," she replied.

Left alone in the waiting area, Jenna picked up her coat from a chair. Every movement took conscious effort as she gathered her bearings.

"Excuse me," a woman said, stepping into the room. Beneath the bangs of her braided black hair, her face shone with concern. "The receptionist told me the family was waiting in here—the Porters. Did you happen to see anyone come by?"

She had to be Reece's sister. What was her name? "They just went to Estelle's room. She's doing great, by the way."

The woman sighed, hand over her chest. "I'm so relieved."

In the beat that followed, her blue eyes clouded with confusion. "I hope this doesn't sound rude, but . . . who are you?" It was a reasonable question.

"Sorry. I'm Jenna Matthews." She thought better of describing her professional role, this not being an ideal time to discuss an estate sale. "I take it you must be Lisa," she suddenly remembered.

"Me?" A small laugh. "Oh, no. I'm Tracy."

Jenna accepted a handshake before Tracy added, "I'm Reece's girlfriend."

It took every ounce of Jenna's will to uphold her smile. Through the instant drought of her throat, she managed to push out, "Of course."

They released hands and Jenna went straight to gripping her coat. She averted her eyes, feeling as transparent as glass. "I should get out of the way. I'm sure if you ask somebody, they can help you find the Porters."

As Jenna started to leave, Tracy asked, "Would you like me to tell them anything for you?"

Jenna shook her head. What more could she possibly say?

Chapter 10

With every step, Reece grew more leery of the scene that awaited in Room 303. The beeping of monitors and scent of disinfectant revived a painfully clear vision. He could still see his grandfather, lying in a hospital bed, the family gathered around to bid farewell.

Now at his grandma's door, Reece welcomed the contrast. She was fully awake and propped upright in an automated bed. His worries melted away as he kissed her on the cheek. On his grandma's other side stood his mom. His dad gave a brief greeting, then went to consult a doctor, not one to trust Reece's recount. What else was new?

Reece shut out the thought and asked, "Are you feeling better?"

"Oh, I'm fine," his grandma said. "Nothing to get riled up about." She waved her hand dismissively, a contradiction to her IV cord and the slightly sluggish motion suggestive of pain meds. "How soon can we leave? Place is chockful of germs."

His mom asserted, "They need to confirm everything's okay first."

"I already told the doc, I'm fit as a fiddle."

After the episode in the car, Reece wasn't about to let her think she could jet out of here without final clearance. "That's what you say now, Grandma. But you weren't that way an hour ago."

"Jeez, Louise. Can't a grown woman have a minor episode without creating a major fuss? When your daddy was little, someone would yell 'boo' and he'd wet his pants. It didn't mean I'd hold him hostage."

"You're not being held hostage," his mom argued. "You're in a hospital."

"Yeah, well. They both poke and prod ya, force you to eat tasteless slop, and charge you a ransom." She turned to Reece. "You be the judge."

He couldn't help but laugh.

Though his mother's mouth twitched from a near smile, she arched a brow at him: *Don't encourage her.* From a plastic pitcher she poured a cup of water and handed it to his grandma.

Having people around to assist the elderly woman, Reece acknowledged, could prove helpful rather than hindering. Unfortunately, the trade-off of that change would be another *I told you so* from his father. Reece's mood declined at the notion. "Do you want me to take Grandma home after they discharge her?"

"Your dad and I can do that, sweetheart. Her room at our place is ready for her to move back in." She brushed a piece of lint from the edge of the blanket and asked his grandma, "How about something to eat?"

"So long as it's not Jell-O or bread pudding. No sense wasting my teeth while I still have them."

His mom rolled her eyes, yet gave in to a smile. "Be right back."

Once she'd left the room, Reece heard a release in his

grandma's breath. Her shoulders sank into the pillow, as though tired from keeping up a show.

He took a seat on the edge of the bed and leaned toward her. "How are you really feeling, Grandma?"

Her lips tightened. The morning seemed to replay in her mind, adding a subtle hoarseness to her voice. "I'll be all right, dear." She lifted her chin and tenderly pinched his cheek. A gesture of love, and thanks. Her inner strength was remarkable.

Reflecting on Jenna's claims, Reece wanted to probe, to learn how far that strength extended. But now wasn't the time.

"Is there anything I can do for you?" he asked.

"Besides breaking me out of here?"

"Besides that."

She considered this. "You can give me the clicker, I suppose. If I have to sit around doing nothing, might as well watch *Wheel of Fortune*."

He grabbed the remote from a nearby chair and passed it along. "I didn't realize you still watched that."

"Just the reruns."

"Isn't that cheating? To already know the answers?"

"Not if you're too senile to remember." She gave him a wink and started flipping through the channels. "Dear, would you go see what your mother's scrounging up? Last thing I need is a bowl of mashed peas. A ham sandwich would be nice."

"I think I can handle that much."

He managed to smile until he made it into the hallway and around the corner. Beneath a swoop of red and green garland, he leaned against a wall, exhausted by the day's roller coaster, its steep drops of *what ifs*. Emotional jostling from another near loss slammed into his chest.

He blew out a breath, regrouping. About to resume his mission, he heard his name from the side.

His father.

"Nurse said Tracy's looking for you."

"Tracy is here?" Then Reece remembered. He'd used a hospital phone, left her a message. "Where is she?"

"In the waiting area where I found you," he said, "with the estate gal." Disapproval edged his voice.

"Look. Nothing happened with us."

"If you say so."

"Jenna was just there, at the house, and—" He stopped, threw his palms up. "You know what? Doesn't matter. You're gonna sit in judgment no matter what I say." He strode past his father to continue down the hall.

"*Reece.*" An order.

If Reece ignored him, would it be worth it? What story would Tracy hear?

He turned back and faced a silent glower. It was obvious what the guy wanted. After all this time, might as well get it over with. "Fine. You were right. You've won, okay?"

His father cocked his head. "Won?"

"About Grandma living alone, about my crazy stunts. You wanted me to play it safe, that's what I'm doing. Anything that involves a risk, it's gone. I'm living the way you've always wanted. So, yeah. You've won."

"Now, you hold on. I don't tell you how to live your life."

"Oh, really?" A prime example rushed into Reece's mind. "How about after the accident?"

His dad shook his head, as if straining to reassemble the memories. Reece, on the other hand, could recall every word, every syllable his father had spewed at that hospital. With the recollection came guilt and shame and resentment from that day.

"After we crashed, I thought I'd killed Tracy. Did you know that?"

The knot on his dad's forehead tightened further.

"At the hospital, her family hated me, and they had every right to. But when *you* got there, more than anything I needed your support. Not a lecture about how badly I'd screwed up. That's something I was well aware of."

His father opened his mouth but, to Reece's surprise, stalled on any retort.

"Excuse me, gentlemen." The nurse who had escorted them from the waiting room reappeared. "We have to keep the volume down in here."

Neither of them replied.

"You're welcome to take the conversation outside." It wasn't a suggestion.

"That's all right," Reece answered, tearing his gaze from his father. "We're finished."

Chapter 11

The house was empty.

Jenna scanned the half-filled boxes in the family room, the countless items needing to be inventoried and tagged. According to Terrence's voicemail, he'd taken the crew home, uncomfortable working today with the client's health in jeopardy.

In the industry, he was one of the compassionate ones. Plenty of liquidators would have charged straight through. The longer you're in the business, the more hardened you're supposed to get. It's about sales, not people. Simplifying, not complicating. Purging, not collecting. It's about getting the job done—which clearly wasn't happening. Two weeks from the estate sale, and thanks to the holidays, they were barely making a dent.

Terrence had made the right decision. But that didn't stop Jenna's frustration from mounting. She snagged a dried-up potted plant she'd meant to toss earlier and dropped it into a black trash bag. From a nearby cabinet she yanked out a stack of games. Their cardboard containers were disintegrating from use. No point checking for missing pieces. Parcheesi, Hangman, Battleship, chess. One after the other, she dumped them all. A deck of Skip-Bo cards spilled over the floor.

She groaned. "Wonderful."

On her knees, she snatched them by the handful. She pitched them into the bag, faster and harder with each scoop. This was her own fault; she had let the job get too personal. Estelle's shoebox, which she'd brought in from her trunk, would be next on the list. She'd sell what she could and toss the rest.

Out with the clutter, she reminded herself. Life was easier without it. Her exchange today with Reece Porter had only confirmed that.

The guy had sent her emotions into a jumbled spiral, and why? Fact was, she barely knew him. He'd certainly never denied having a girlfriend. Nonetheless, a feeling of betrayal swelled inside. Worse yet, of being no better than her father's mistress.

The thought was irrational. Just like the tears building behind her eyes. Pushing them down, she reached under the sofa to gather the stray cards. A 9 was just beyond her reach, like so many other things these days.

Lying on her side, she stretched out her arm. Almost . . . had it . . .

The doorbell chimed. Reflexively, her finger flicked the card away. Jenna fumed as the bell rang again. Her parked van likely boosted the caller's hope in summoning a person. Soon, persistence would lead to an annoying series of knocks.

Jenna marched toward the entry and swung open the door. "Yes?"

An elderly man stood under the portico, out of the rain. He wore a damp trench coat over his suit and navy bow tie, a fedora hat shielding his eyes. His silver mustache was narrow and neatly trimmed.

"Pardon me, miss. I hope I'm not bothering you." He spoke with such tenderness Jenna swiftly reined in her emotions.

"Not at all. What can I do for you?"

"I saw an ad for the estate sale with this address. Said it was for the Porters."

She should have guessed. Estates with well-known owners tended to attract sneak peeks.

"I'm sorry, but we're not having a preview on this house. If you'd like to come back on December seventeenth—"

"I'm not here for the sale. I . . ." The man removed his hat and squeezed it to the medium frame of his chest. "I just need to know if Stella . . ." He inhaled a breath before the rest tumbled out coarsely. "Has she passed?"

Stella?

"Do you mean Estelle Porter?" Considering the topic, clarity was essential.

He mustered a nod as Jenna realized the implication that had drawn him here. Estate sales for elderly residents commonly followed a death. From the stranger's intensity, Jenna was even more grateful the day's emergency had ended as it did.

"Mrs. Porter is alive and well," she told him. "She's simply moving in with her family."

A gasp shot from the man's lips, which suddenly quivered. Same for his hands. "Thank you," he breathed. "That's . . . thank you."

Dazed, he fumbled in replacing his hat and started to leave. An old Chevy sat empty in the driveway, streaked with raindrops. The last thing Jenna needed was another distraction, but she couldn't let him operate a car in his unsettled state, especially with the slick, winding roads in the area. One hospital run was enough for the day.

"Sir," she called out, "why don't you come inside?"

He angled a quarter of the way back, then raised a hand. "I'd better not. I wouldn't want to intrude."

"It's just me here, and I'd love the company."

The man hesitated, contemplating.

"Please," she said, growing weary. "Just until the rain lets up."

He glanced at the road, his car, the house. With a small nod, he agreed.

"Do you live around here?" Jenna asked, padding the silence as she waited for the microwave to beep.

The man sat in his chair, fingering the brim of his hat on the Formica table. "Summerville Center."

"Oh, sure. Over in Tigard." Two of Jenna's former clients had moved into the retirement home. "Seems like a nice place to live."

He smiled softly.

At last, she delivered the heated mug. He steeped his tea bag by lifting and dropping it several times.

"So," Jenna said, "you've known Estelle—or Stella, for a long time?"

He took a sip before replying. "It was quite some years ago."

Silence again.

She debated on excusing herself and returning to task, but intrigue, her greatest enemy lately, baited her to stay. "I'm Jenna, by the way. And you are . . . ?"

Inclining his head, he accepted her handshake. His light blue eyes held a charming if worn twinkle. "Tom."

As she watched him take another sip, his look of discomfort growing, the connection sank in. Still, there had to be a million Toms out there.

"I really ought to be going," he said.

When it came to Jenna's work, there had always been lines, unspoken but clear. Yet after a week with the Porters, those lines were blurring. And now, with the man's departure imminent, any rules ceased to exist.

Rising, he donned his hat.

"Are you Corporal Redding?" she blurted.

He froze, his eyes downcast. An infinite pause stretched the air taut until he spoke. "Stella told you about me?"

"Well . . . she . . ." Jenna had to confess, "No. Not exactly."

His gaze lifted, swirling with disappointment, confusion. He wanted to know if he'd been forgotten. Jenna understood the feeling, from her father. And she refused to let this kindhearted man believe the memory of him was lost.

"Mr. Redding," she said, coming to her feet, "I have something to show you."

In the den, Jenna led Tom around an obstacle of hand trucks and moving supplies. She guided him to sit in the cushioned swivel chair. Forbidding herself a second thought, she presented the shoebox.

Slowly, he pulled out the photographs and laid them on the desk. His expression lightened by degrees until, as with Estelle, the decades since the war vanished from his face.

"It was just yesterday," he murmured.

"This is you, then, with the mistletoe." It wasn't a question, just an observance of a mystery being solved.

He touched that particular picture and sported a boyish grin. "Had to get creative. I was bound and determined to get a smooch out of that girl."

Jenna smiled along with him, feeling as if she had been there. "And did it work?"

Tom shook his head. "Only on the cheek. Consorting like that was against the rules." He let out a soft laugh. "Course, she found me later behind the supply tent and gave me a kiss I'll never forget. Blew my army socks clear off."

"So . . . you two started dating?"

"Well. Not officially."

No elaboration. Perhaps he preferred a less intimate topic.

Jenna retrieved from the box another piece of the puzzle. The enclosed Bronze Star. As she flipped open the case, he tilted his head. "Ahh, yeah," he sighed.

"Do you know how she got this?"

He hummed in affirmation, running his thumb over the grooves of the medal. "We were stationed in Dutch New Guinea at the time. MacArthur was leapfrogging toward Tokyo. Docs and nurses were being rotated up to the front. Stella volunteered to help, which I didn't like one bit. And I sure as heck told her so."

"But she went anyway," Jenna guessed.

Tom glanced up, brow raised. "One thing about Stella. She was the sweetest girl you ever met. But make no mistake, few people were better at holding their ground." A mix of frustration and admiration seeped into his voice. "Turned out to be a good thing, anyhow. She saved a whole lot of soldiers out there."

After a moment, Tom set down the award. He straightened, prompting Jenna to do the same. He was going to leave. But he couldn't. Not yet. A buried tale was surfacing. All that was left in the box, however, was a tattered book.

A last ditch effort, she hastened to hold up *Jane Eyre.* "Any idea if this was special to her?"

Tom stared for several seconds. His skin paled. As he sank into his chair, any remnants of nostalgic warmth drained away. He handled the book as though poison soaked its pages. On the inside cover was an inscription Jenna could just make out from her angle.

My darling, Merry Christmas!
Tom

Shoulders hunched, he shut his eyes. "That's all I could come up with," he said before forcing another look.

Jenna simply waited, not pushing.

"It was her favorite novel," he finally added. "I spent a good half hour trying to write a thoughtful note, and that was it. No mention of love. No gratitude for taking care of me." He shook his head as tears welled. "I was so angry at the world. It was never her, of course, but that's who I took it out on."

Jenna was struggling to keep up when he gazed at her intently, a plea for understanding.

"We were being shipped home, from the Philippines. War was over. People were celebrating for days. With all the commotion it took me a minute to even realize I'd been hit."

The way he spoke the word, Jenna gathered the meaning. "You were shot?"

"Some drunken GI had fired off a pistol. Got me right in the kneecap. That's why we held off marrying. I told Stella I wouldn't go down that aisle till I could walk nice and smooth. That's how dumb and stubborn I was."

The tragic irony was staggering to Jenna. Serving in a world war, only to be wounded by your own side. And all while celebrating America's victory.

"Did you . . . break up because of your injury?"

"If it weren't for an infection, things might've been different. But you see, I couldn't work for some time. And alcohol helped dull the pain." He clutched the book as he continued. "Back then, being a man meant earning a paycheck. You couldn't have a woman doing it for you. Wartime was one thing, but back at home, life was supposed to be normal. Besides, Stella was too good for that. I promised I'd take care of her, and somehow it all got turned around. I actually had myself convinced it'd be a relief for us both when we went our separate ways."

Estelle's efforts to break from the past began to make sense. Jenna's soap-opera theories fizzled on the spot.

Tom released the book. He attempted to flatten the edges he'd bent. "Important thing is, when I happened across her husband's obituary, listing their kids and grandkids, I knew she'd had a good life. Just like I had with Noreen—God rest her. So really, it all worked out for the best."

"Had you ever thought about contacting Stella? To tell her all of this?"

He stifled a small laugh. "Wrote half a dozen versions of a letter over the years. In the end, always felt like nudging a beehive. Didn't seem right to disturb her life."

Jenna nodded, relating to the intent. The couple's circumstances, though, had changed. "Maybe it's time to mail one of those letters."

His gaze dropped to the photos. He shrugged a shoulder and said, "Oh . . . I don't know . . ."

"Mr. Redding, you came here today, worrying it was too late. But now you know it's not."

"Yeah, well. We'll see." His tone didn't sound promising.

He patted the book, a farewell motion, and rose to his feet. "I'd really best get going."

"Are you sure? There's really no reason to rush."

"Nah, nah. I've taken up enough of your time."

She yielded with reluctance and walked him to the door, where they traded holiday tidings. He was a few steps outside when he pivoted back. "Miss," he said, "I want to thank you for that."

Thanks for what? For allowing Jenna to pry open old wounds?

"I really didn't do anything you should be grateful for." His lips curved into a wistful smile that argued otherwise.

Chapter 12

Although part of him still resisted the change, Reece had to admit the setup was better than he'd expected. In the basement of his parents' house, the walls of his old bedroom had always been the color of stone. Fitting for a teenager, it had provided a brooding backdrop for posters of rock groups and rebel athletes. The feeling of being separate from the house had made it an ideal spot during high school.

He rotated slowly now, hardly recognizing the space. A fresh coat of buttery yellow paint had transformed the dungeon into a cozy cove. A miniature kitchen appeared where a storage closet once stood. Best of all, elements of his grandma's home were sprinkled throughout: a mounted shelf of porcelain figurines; down bedding and a claw-footed hope chest; floral curtains that virtually matched her own.

Below the two windows, his grandma sat in her rocking chair, sifting through Christmas cards forwarded from her old house. A tasseled lamp glowed on the nightstand, brightening her pallor. She looked remarkably better than she did in the hospital. Hard to believe that was only four days ago.

Reece held up the poinsettias, the pot wrapped in a silver bow. "A little housewarming gift for you."

She flicked them but a glance. "Lovely, dear."

In the notable quiet, he set the plant on her dresser, another furnishing from her house.

"Why didn't Dad ever say he was going to fix it up like this?" Reece said this more to himself than to her.

"Could be that you never asked."

True. Although he couldn't imagine asking his father much of anything at the moment. Thankfully, the guy was holed up in his garage, making it easy for Reece to slip in and out before dinner.

From upstairs wafted the aroma of baked crescent rolls. The slight trace of burnt dough delivered an idea.

"You know, with you being here now, Mom can finally pick up some cooking tips."

After a halfhearted smile, his grandma continued to study her cards in an absent manner. Adjusting to a new way of life was never easy. Quiet time to dwell often made things worse.

"Hey, how about some music?" He turned the knob of her antique RCA radio. He'd forgotten how touchy those dials were to find a station without static. At last, an FM channel projected a clear tune, "Grandma Got Run Over by a Reindeer." The repetitive chorus tended to grind at his nerves, but he hoped the lyrics might give her a giggle. Which they didn't.

He was grateful the song ended, until he registered the next one: "I'll Be Home for Christmas." He clicked the radio off.

"Mom says she's set aside an area in the backyard so you can garden in the spring."

His grandma murmured her acknowledgment.

"Also, I hear some of your friends have been calling to check on you. I think they've been hoping you'll join their quilting group again."

He waited for a wisecrack about hanging out with blind old biddies. But nothing came.

Reece couldn't stand seeing her this way. He understood where she was; he'd been there before himself. And it was his grandma's no-nonsense advice that had ultimately yanked him out of his cave. Serving up that same tidbit to her now, about throwing a solo pity party, was tempting. Unfortunately, he doubted his own ability to deliver the words with his grandma's charm.

He perched on the end of her hope chest, wishing he possessed a magic formula to revive the strong grandmother he knew.

He'd done his best to stamp out thoughts of Jenna the last several days—the powdery fragrance of her skin, how close he'd come to kissing her and, once again, screwing up his life—but at this moment, her assurances returned with unavoidable clarity. She'd seemed certain of his grandmother's courage, all based on a past Reece knew nothing about. It could be helpful, reminding his grandma of her younger days, when her military service required independence and bravery.

He clasped his hands, elbows on his knees, and leaned closer. "Jenna Matthews—the gal working at your house—she told me about a box she found. Things you saved from the war."

His grandma's hands went still. Her gaze remained on her lap.

"Is it true you served in an army hospital?"

Her silence served as confirmation, along with the sense that she'd hoped to keep that nugget under wraps. But why? Why the cover-up, the lies?

"At first, I told Jenna she had to be mistaken. That you'd even said you'd never been to Asia before."

"Vacationed," she corrected boldly, and raised her head. "I said I never *vacationed* there. Aside from a few coconut cocktails, it wasn't exactly Club Med."

One could argue it a technicality, but at least she wasn't denying the claim.

"I don't get it," he said. "Being an army nurse is something you should be proud of. Why didn't you ever mention it?" Reece could see vets not wanting to share details, given how gruesome he imagined the war had been, but not hiding their service altogether.

"Please, Grandma," he insisted gently. "Just between us. You can tell me about it."

Following a lengthy pause, she looked into his eyes and appeared to recognize her own stubbornness—meaning Reece wasn't about to let the subject go.

She sat back in her chair and set her cards aside. Then she sighed, as if dusting off stored-up words. "We weren't nurses," she clarified. "That would have taken a lot more training than enlisting in the WAC, and I was too eager to do my bit. Once there, of course, we took to their duties all the same."

"So you *were* stationed in the jungle?"

"It was nothing like *Gilligan's Island*, I can tell you that much. After a few days in Hollandia, we sure didn't resemble Ginger or Mary Ann." She let out a small laugh. "You should have seen my parents' reaction. About had a conniption over my appearance when I got home. It only supported why they were against me joining up in the first place."

"And that's why you never talked about it," Reece concluded, still trying to understand.

"It wasn't just them. Society's never been a fan of change, dear. Once we came back, I learned real fast that putting WAC on a résumé was a surefire way *not* to get hired. The soldiers we'd helped, they knew the truth, but most people at home preferred to believe we'd helped boost morale in . . . well, in other ways."

Reece got the point, along with her motivation for secrecy.

Shame dictated she close that chapter of her life as though it had never happened.

"Then, years later," she said, eyes glimmering behind her glasses, "I met your grandfather. Together we created a family I couldn't be prouder of." She paused before reaching over to pat Reece's forearm. "Way I see it, better to focus on the path ahead, rather than hanging on to what's already done."

Her pointed remark wasn't lost on him. Clearly, she had overheard him and his father bickering at the hospital. Considering their volume, how could she have avoided it? Maybe Reece was long overdue to drop the weights of his own past. "I hear what you're saying, Grandma," he conceded.

But then, recalling where this conversation began, he sent the lesson right back at her. "Who knows, I might even get the itch to join a quilting group. Visit old friends, start cooking, gardening. That kind of thing."

She pursed her lips, fighting a smile that ultimately won out. "How on earth did you become such a smart aleck?"

"Must be hereditary."

"Must be."

As they laughed together, the room gained an even cozier feel. That's precisely how it remained through the rest of their chat, which shifted to lighter topics. It went unspoken that their thoughts and emotions needed a break. And so, they engaged in the usual discussions of books and weather and *Wheel of Fortune*.

At a natural lull, their talk having run its course, Reece prepared to leave. He stood and gave her a soft peck on the cheek.

"Wait, before you go," she said, gesturing toward her jewelry box. "Got something for you in the bottom drawer."

It didn't dawn on him what that something would be until he grabbed the knob. A velvet ring box stared back at him.

"You still wanted that, didn't you, dear?"

He creaked open the case. Inside, a small marquise diamond topped a beautiful silver band. Amazing how a whole future could rest on such a small object.

Reece turned to his grandma, replying with a smile. Time to live without regrets.

Chapter 13

Jenna shifted in her seat, a director's chair, fending off the urge to fidget. Lightbulbs framing the mirror compounded the heat generated by her nerves. She should have skipped her morning latte. The caffeine was proving anything but soothing.

Mia, the makeup artist, pulled a comb from the apron tied around her hefty middle. Candy cane earrings shimmered beside her elaborate black braids, her skin flawlessly smooth. "Okay if I touch up your hair?" she asked, aerosol already in hand.

"Spray away." Jenna pinned on a smile, which she dropped once she felt her cheeks tremble. A guest spot on a talk show had sounded utterly exciting. But after arriving early at the station, the producer had put such stress on the live-air aspect of *Good Day Northwest*, Jenna now feared being a tongue-tied disaster. It didn't help that her mother had told everyone on the planet about the program.

"Been on the show before?" Mia asked while launching a shower of hairspray.

Jenna coughed on a mouthful and shook her head.

"Well then, I'll make sure you look fabulous for your debut. You're talking about used jewelry, right?"

"Right," Jenna squeezed out.

Mia de-shined Jenna's face with a brush full of powder. "Buying or selling it?"

Once the air cleared enough, Jenna said, "Both."

Their fractured conversation resembled visits with her dental hygienist, who never failed to ask a question when Jenna's mouth was stuffed with cotton, cardboard, or bubble gum fluoride. As the current exchange trudged along, she tried not to grimace at the heavy application of red lipstick and rosy blush—although her mother would be thrilled. Jenna repeatedly reminded herself that the studio lights washed out color.

"Don't know about you," Mia remarked, "but I couldn't do it."

A pointed pause hauled Jenna back to the discussion. "I'm sorry . . . ?"

"Wear a divorced person's ring. Or even a hawked engagement band, for that matter. Just so much sadness and turmoil tied to those kinda things."

Jenna countered with her usual: "Yes, but they could bring a lot of happiness to the new buyer."

"I don't know, maybe . . ." Mia worked at taming a lock of Jenna's shag. "Then again, I'm more of the sentimental type. Every spring I vow to clean out my daughter's art projects from school, now with her off at college, but just can't bring myself to do it."

Jenna easily visualized the boxes, crammed with wrinkled handprint paintings and glitter-shedding snowflakes—none of which would be viewed more than twice.

"What about you?" Mia asked with another quick spray. If she was perpetuating conversation to ease a nervous guest, the attempt was failing.

"I don't have kids."

"No, I meant is there anything you collect?"

That word again. "There's nothing."

"Oh, surely there's something you cherish enough to hang on to."

Jenna shook her head against the disbelief that blared in Mia's tone. Why was the concept so hard to get? "I am *not* a collector."

Mia paused the primping, fist on her hip. She was only making small talk. When had Jenna become so neurotic?

In the stiffening silence, the woman sharpened an eyebrow pencil.

Jenna searched for a way to backpedal before Mia added, "Way I see it, we're all collectors in one way or another. Keepers of memories, if nothing else. Some aren't as pretty as others, but wipe out one half and you'd lose the other . . ."

As her words trailed off, Tom Redding's face appeared in Jenna's mind. Wrinkles at the corners of his eyes, as well as his mouth, bespoke smiles and frowns, happy and sad moments, like the memories in Estelle's box.

That darn haunting box.

Jenna still couldn't bring herself to throw the thing away, yet she should have. Life had been easier before its complicating ties. Disposing of others' items had always brought relief—at least until the craving returned. Which it always did. Like an addiction, some might say. Like cigarettes or alcohol, or . . . hoarding.

"Miss Matthews?" The intern who'd initially greeted Jenna poked her head in from the greenroom. "We're ready for you."

Jenna sprang from her chair, thankful for the interruption.

"Not just yet," Mia ordered, filling Jenna with dread. Had the woman somehow read her thoughts?

Mia merely removed the protective tissues she'd tucked into the collar of Jenna's sweater, which the producer had borrowed from the "emergency wardrobe" closet for a more festive look than her own muted ensemble.

Jenna reviewed herself in the mirror. Between the bright red garment and matching lipstick, she felt like a Rudolph the Red-lipped Reindeer.

"Right this way," the intern said. She led Jenna down the same hall she'd traversed earlier to set up her display.

Again, they wove through the station's maze, past editing rooms with walls of monitors and enough buttons and switches for a NASA control center. With a wave of the girl's badge over a security pad, an alarm beeped once and the door opened.

"Watch your step," she said as they approached an obstacle course of thick black cords. Each was connected to one of several mounted cameras facing the vacant news anchors' desk. A solid green wall denoted the meteorologist's area. Reporting the winter weather in Portland—rain, drizzle, downpour—had to be as thrilling as reporting sunshine in Arizona. The intern held a finger to her lips, a warning to Jenna that the microphones were "hot." In the studio kitchen, the host, whose former role as a sportscaster befit his appearance, was sampling a Cajun twist on Christmas turkey. Judging from the sweat beading on his forehead, the meat had fully absorbed the chef 's Southern spice.

When the show broke for a commercial, a floor director clipped Jenna's mike in place, then rushed her to the table of jewelry. Jenna had borrowed some from her boss, some from coworkers; others she'd snagged from a pawnshop. The host threw her a quick hello before guzzling water from a glass and flipping through his note cards. The female floor director launched a countdown. A cameraman gripped his handles as he spoke into his headset while the other camera moved on its own.

Amid the chaos of the room, Jenna's ears heated. She smoothed her hair over both lobes, praying they weren't the same shade as her sweater.

Focus on the table, she told herself. She would work her way from left to right, just as she'd practiced, starting with a gemmed bracelet that only needed a few minor repairs to double its value.

"We're live in five, four . . ." The floor director continued silently with three fingers. Two. One. Then a red light glowed on the camera as she pointed to the host.

"Welcome back to *Good Day Northwest*," he said, standing beside Jenna. "'Tis the season of gift giving. If your pocketbook is a little light this year, not to worry. Used jewelry could save the day. Here to tell us how is Jenna Matthews, an estate liquidator who's built a career on pricing and selling off other people's treasures."

Jenna winced. Yeah, the description was true, technically, but it sounded terrible stated that way.

"Thanks for being on the show." He smiled at her, but she could see in his eyes that he'd rather be talking about touchdowns than trinkets.

"Thanks for having me."

"To start off, why don't you tell our viewers how determining the value of jewelry can come in handy at Christmastime?"

"Well," she said, recalling her rehearsed speech, "if you understand how to appraise a piece acquired at an estate sale or a flea market, for example, you'll know what you're actually giving someone. It's also helpful when you're selling jewelry you already own."

"And those proceeds can be used to buy other gifts," he finished.

"That's right."

"Sounds dollar-smart to me. I bet there's lots of collectors out there who have a drawerful gathering dust. My wife, for one." He winked at the camera.

The vision of a drawer invaded Jenna's thoughts. If she were given even half of one to fill, what would she put inside? All she had collected was empty space. A preventative measure, it created a barrier against anything that might hurt her. The flip side was that nothing meaningful could get through.

"So, let's get started," the host went on. He gestured to the brooch on the right side of the table. "How about this pin? What would that go for?"

Pin? He was supposed to start with the left. The bracelet! At home, over and over she had practiced in that order. Pores of perspiration opened on her scalp as her mind reeled in search of the value.

Think, think . . .

The Victorian brooch was an heirloom. Terrence's mother had given it to him the Christmas before she passed. Not to wear himself, of course, but to keep in the family. He let Jenna borrow it, claiming his mom would have loved showing it off. He said that as a kid he used to believe the ivory profile was fashioned after his mom.

"Just a ballpark figure," the host prompted, alerting Jenna that she hadn't responded.

"I would say . . ." she began. "The value would be . . ."

The guy flickered an intense glance at the floor director, a plea for help with his stage-frightened guest.

Jenna hastened to calculate, to estimate anything close. Then another image came to her: Estelle's Bronze Star. From it, a sudden peacefulness flowed, for there was only one true answer.

"It's priceless."

Covering with a smile, the host flashed another side glance. "I'm sure to the owner it is. But what do you think the dollar range would be?"

"Really . . . there isn't one."

"Excuse me?"

The revelation struck like electricity, humming through her veins. How could anyone put a price tag on a woman's final gift to her son? It could be a dried dandelion or a piece of string, and no dollar amount would do it justice. The same applied, she realized, to a kid's baseball caught with his grandpa.

Confidence growing, Jenna explained, "Perception is what dictates price—whether it's of paintings and furnishings or an-

THE CHRISTMAS COLLECTOR / 83

tiques and jewelry. That's a basic standard for any type of retail. It's what says a store can charge eight dollars, or eight hundred, for a pair of shoes. All that said," she confessed, "what I hadn't understood, for a long time now, was the major role memories play in that perception."

"Uh, yes," the host interjected, "I see what you mean." His uncertainty over the segment's direction tolled as loud as church bells.

Jenna, on the other hand, knew precisely where her message was headed. She turned to the camera and spoke directly to her mother.

"In different ways, we all have voids to fill. Holidays, for a lot of people, can bring those feelings out even more. The best thing we can do is to fill our lives with things that matter, like . . . turning a favorite hobby into a job, or finding a person you're crazy about. Even if none of those things come with guarantees."

The story of Tom and Estelle, despite their relationship's end, exemplified the need to take a risk.

"Allowing people you care about into your life, and letting them know how important they are, that's the best present you can give them." In the brief lull, Jenna glimpsed the wide-eyed host, spurring her to veer back on course. "Which is . . . why a gift of jewelry carries more value, in every aspect, when it's personal and tied to a memory."

At the floor director's cue, the host angled toward the teleprompter. "Definitely a great message for the holidays. Speaking of holidays, after the break Mimi the Elf will teach us how to make ornaments out of plastic toys from fast-food meals, sure to become the talk of the neighborhood." He pushed up a grin. "Don't go away."

The instant the red light turned off, the host's expression made clear his last line wasn't meant for Jenna.

Swept off by the intern, who stole back the microphone, Jenna wound through the station, pausing only to reclaim her blouse and coat. She signed out at the front desk, where a television was now airing Mimi the Elf.

"That was quite a segment," the receptionist said, hands pausing on his keyboard.

"Yeah," Jenna breathed, and handed over her visitor's badge.

"Best one I've seen in a while."

Jenna would have taken the phrase for sarcasm if not for his tone. "Thanks," she said with matching sincerity.

In the parking lot, she inhaled the crisp morning air. Clouds were giving way to a clear sky. Everything about the day felt different.

As she retrieved her keys from her purse, she noticed a message on her phone, a text from her mom: **Loved the show. Loved your sweater. Love you.**

Jenna smiled at the note, reminding her of their conversation from Thanksgiving. Indeed, like a character in a romantic comedy, with a microphone on and the world tuned in, Jenna had been seized by a revelation. There was a good reason, she decided, to declare your stand in public. Because then you couldn't go backward.

Her career would be the next step.

While she still believed in the job's value—helping families, transitioning residents—the idea of price tagging Estelle's effects wrung her stomach. How could she pay her mortgage with another person's memories? No partnership would be worth the trade. If she had to sell her condo, even at a loss, that's undoubtedly what she would do.

The prospect, though scary, thrilled and liberated her—thanks, in part, to Terrence. Of any coworker she knew, he would treat the Porter estate with compassion. She floated on this certainty as she slid into her car, before the buzz of her phone jostled her. She expected to see her mom's number, not Sally's.

"Oh, boy." Jenna braced herself for an earful about her behavior on the show. Needless to say, she didn't foresee another invitation.

"Can you talk?" Sally greeted with urgency.

"Um . . . sure."

"I didn't want to get your hopes up, in case I was wrong. But I just heard back from an old professor of mine in Chicago."

"Wait. What are we talking about?" Obviously, Sally had missed the broadcast.

"The teapot from the Porter estate. I knew it denoted the Qing dynasty, and that the stamp was rare. But I've been fooled by something similar before."

Jenna's thoughts spun as she pictured the small Chinese ceramic. "So . . . you're saying . . ."

Sally replied with a smile in her voice. "Merry Christmas, lady. You hit the jackpot."

Chapter 14

Reece squeezed the side handle, more out of frustration than for safety. Beside him, bundled in winter sporting wear, Tracy steered their golf cart toward the green.

"Uh-oh," she sang out, nose scrunched. She brought them to a stop by the sixth flag. "I think it's in the water."

Big surprise. So far today, his shots had landed him in several sand traps and in knee-high rough. Once on another fairway. His thoughts were frenzied, his muscles the furthest thing from loose. When he'd arranged their golf outing, he hadn't actually planned on them playing a round.

But then, he hadn't banked on Tracy running late to the clubhouse, near frantic they'd miss their tee time. Nor had he foreseen the ranger glowering at them for stalling the game on his watch.

"Hon, I need to talk to you," Reece had told her as they approached the first tee box.

"After this hole, okay?" She'd dashed off to set up with her pitching wedge, ponytail swinging through the back of her Pinnacle cap. Rushing had slightly hooked her drive, causing her to mutter a few choice words. Not an ideal moment to pop the question.

Still, he'd wanted to follow through. This was, after all, where they had first met—a concept he'd borrowed from her sister's proposal. Plus, for an outdoor girl like Tracy, the mountain backdrop, towering trees, and open air fit her perfectly. The rarity of blue sky on a December day in Oregon, just as forecasted, had seemed a telling sign.

Yet before he could retrieve the ring, tucked into his golf bag, a foursome from the Hit 'n' Giggle club had pulled up for their turn. Armed with visors and Bloody Marys, the boisterous ladies had unknowingly squashed Reece's attempt.

Hole two had become his next option, then three, then four. But no moment had felt right. Reece had sped through his putting to gain privacy from the group. This only worsened his shots, aggravating him more. An ugly cycle. With Christmas just two weeks away, the window of opportunity was narrowing; he refused to attend another Graniello holiday without making things official.

New plan of attack, he told himself, striding toward the water to the left of the green. Pitching wedge and putter in his grip, he surveyed the area, desperate for an idea.

The clubhouse.

Three more holes and they'd be at the halfway mark, a good chance for a lunch break fireside. Whoever said proposing over a Payne Stewart Burger wasn't romantic? Points for uniqueness. They could look back at it one day and laugh.

"Yesss," Tracy exclaimed. Her chip onto the green had placed her ball in an ideal spot. From there it rolled in a gentle curve, almost in slow motion, and ended—*plonk*—in the cup. Her lips stretched with elation before she glanced at Reece. In an instant, she dropped her smile, stifling her celebration.

Compassionate. He mentally added the trait to the list, a

compilation of all the reasons he'd be a moron not to marry the girl.

"Any sign of your ball?" she hollered

He rotated in a circle and shook his head.

Lofty chatter projected from the foursome gaining on them.

"Why don't you just call it a nine?" Tracy suggested. As in, a mercy score so they could skip this hole and move on. Surely, that's how the Bloody Mary gang was playing. With twice as many people, how else were they progressing so fast?

Or were his skills today even more pathetic than he'd gathered?

Reece straightened, pulling back his shoulders. Today, of all days, he needed his ego intact.

"I'll take the drop." He reached into his right pants pocket. Nothing but plastic markers and wooden tees. He patted the other front pocket, then those of his windbreaker. Empty. He'd blown through them all. At this rate, he couldn't even qualify for the Hit 'n' Giggle league.

He spoke through a clenched jaw. "Can you give me an extra?"

"Sure thing." Tracy offered an overly cheery smile. "I'll bring it over."

As he waited for a spare, he studied the murky water that surely had swallowed his ball. In the hint of reflection was a guy who, not so long ago, would have shucked off his spiked shoes, rolled up his pant legs, and waded into that icy water without hesitation.

He rubbed at his temple with his gloved hand, pushing down the thought, and noted Tracy's delay. He raised his head. Rather than mere steps away, she had gone over to their cart. She was searching for a ball in her golf bag.

No, not hers—his. *His bag!*

"Tracy, wait! I'll get it!" He meant to speed-walk in a semi-natural manner but instead burst into a sprint.

Fortunately, his warning worked. She halted any movement until he reached her, at which point she slowly lifted her eyes. The source of their intensity lay in her palm. His grandmother's box. Open. The ring exposed.

"Is this . . ." she said, a wisp of a voice. She didn't finish; she already understood.

Reece took a breath. He envisioned himself kneeling, holding up the ring, and taking her hand. He heard his prepared speech, saw tears fill her eyes, right before she accepted.

This was it. The grandiose moment.

But at the recollection of his grandma's phrase, a condition of passing along the ring—"If you love this girl with all your heart"—his world froze. His legs wouldn't bend and hands wouldn't rise. His speech had crumbled, and the syllables wouldn't adhere.

"Yoo-hoo!" a woman sang out, breaking his paralysis. "Mind if we play through?"

Reece managed to motion his hand in agreement. The ladies flitted their fingers in thanks, then stood there. Waiting. It dawned on him that he and Tracy should move aside if they didn't want a golf ball to the skull. He angled back toward Tracy to guide her away, but she had disappeared. His heart pounded like a fist to the chest.

He scanned the area until catching sight of her. She'd found a park bench off to the side, an empty space often used for the snack cart. She was staring down at the ring that glinted in the sunlight, but her expression wasn't the kind that preceded happy tears.

Reece forced down a swallow of confusion, offense, relief. Hands balled at his sides, he made his way over and lowered himself beside her.

Not looking up, she said, "Reece, you don't want to propose to me."

His lips parted, an effort to craft a denial—that refused to come. She was right. And hearing the sentiment aloud confirmed it all the more. Nevertheless, he cared for her deeply and hated that his behavior might have hurt her.

"I think it's obvious what's been going on," she told him. "It's finally time we talked about it."

A million thoughts swarmed him. Cautious, he said, "Okay . . ."

She set down the ring box and peered into his eyes. "After I went to the hospital and met that girl you were with, that's when I knew for sure."

Jenna Matthews . . . that's what this was about?

He'd had a feeling his father was going to blab for no good reason. "I barely know her. You have to believe me."

"I do believe you." Tracy's reply, firm and calm, stopped the revving of his defenses.

"Then . . . what?"

She shook her head and gazed toward the passing carts. "When Jenna and I met in the waiting room, I introduced myself as your girlfriend. She tried to hide it, but it was obvious she was disappointed."

Given the chaos of that day, Reece hadn't considered the two of them crossing paths. God, Jenna must have taken him for a—

He snipped off the thought. His history with Tracy took precedence, everything they had endured as a team.

"That doesn't matter," he insisted. He reached out and held her hand, regaining her attention.

"It does if you're not sure about us."

"What? No, but I am."

"But if you weren't—"

"Sweetheart, you don't have to worry. Remember, I promised I'd take care of you."

"Yes, I know that." Her voice gained a graveled edge. "But that's not a reason to stay together."

"What are you talking about? There are other things—"

"Reece," she burst out, "I was planning to break up with you."

His mind did a double take. He pulled his hand away. Like the ring, he'd become unwittingly exposed.

At last, she shifted her body to face him, softening. "I liked you, Reece, from the minute we met. You were unpredictable and loads of fun. But we were really different." She quickened her pace, sounding tense from effort. "We'd only been dating a few months. I was going to move on, but then the accident happened. You were so wonderful, sticking by me . . . ."

The reality of their past hurtled through Reece's head. It rattled his core before gradually settling in. "And guilt's kept us together," he finished.

After a heavy pause, Tracy nodded. "I think you're a great guy, I really do. We're just not meant to be together like this," she said. "Honestly, I think we've both been pretending to be something we're not."

The scenario was certainly a familiar one. His grandmother, all from a shame of her own, had spent decades hiding part of herself, playing things safe to please others. Even now, she deserved to live her life, not watch it pass by.

The same could be said about him, he supposed.

"So," Reece sighed.

"So," Tracy echoed.

"What do you say we call it a day?" His reference addressed much more than the game, which naturally went without saying.

She smiled in thoughtful agreement. Her eyes misted over as they relaxed into the quiet.

"Still friends?" she asked.

Whether they would be or not, he didn't know for sure. But

he did know they would always share a piece of each other's past.

"Get over here," he encouraged, motioning with his chin. When she scooted closer, he layered his arm over her shoulders and rested his cheek on her head.

On the bench beside them remained his grandma's ring. Light bounced off the diamond, as if sending a wink.

Chapter 15

Anticipation thrummed as Jenna waited for the big unveiling. Seated in the reception area, she glimpsed her reflection in a window. On the daring scale, her fresh, cherry Coke highlights were nothing compared to the transformation taking place across the salon.

Once again, she flipped through the magazine featuring the new look her mother had chosen for herself. The hairstylist was so eager to get started, intent on sending the frizzy bangs back to the eighties, that she barely glanced at the example.

"It'll look fabulous," Jenna had said, detecting second thoughts in her mother's eyes. Jenna was still astounded her mom had initiated the appointment, a tough yet much-needed decision. Just like Jenna's career.

According to Sally, the teapot boasted a value upward of forty grand. The single antique piece would have ensured Jenna's partnership—at the cost of her conscience. *I'm not being stupid, I'm not being stupid*, she'd told herself, entering her boss's office. Quitting anything went against Jenna's nature, but finishing the job would have been a step backward, above all tempting her to continue a chapter of her life in need of closing. And when she walked away, she'd felt a burden lift.

"You can come see her now," the receptionist announced, her stature compact and tone raspy.

Jenna tossed the magazine aside and followed with the anxiousness of a father about to view his newborn.

"She's over there." The receptionist pointed toward the farthest hair station before skittering away. Jenna hoped that wasn't a sign the gal was taking cover.

Past wafts of styling sprays and chemical dyes, Jenna threaded through the room. Hair dryers boomed, mimicking a 747 at takeoff. In the corner, a row of hunched manicurists tended to women with fancy updos. Sparkly hair clips and berry red polish screamed of holiday parties.

Finally, Jenna hooked gazes with the stylist. If her mom hated the results, there would be no second attempt.

In a magician's move, the stylist yanked off her customer's cape and swiveled the chair one-eighty, presenting her creation.

Jenna gasped. She just . . . couldn't believe . . .

Her mother's brow knotted in fear. "You don't like it."

On a solid note of honesty, Jenna shook her head. "Nope," she told her. "I *love* it."

Her mom giggled in relief. Like a little girl wobbling in heels, an air of excitement outweighed her uncertainty. She touched the shortened sides that ran just below her jawline, sloping longer toward the front. All frizz and gray had been banished from her sleek, straightened hair.

Jenna added, "And Doobie will love it even more."

Her mom brushed off the comment, betrayed by her reddening cheeks. Already, Jenna could see the awe in his face while picking her mother up for their weekly lesson. Personally, Jenna wasn't a fan of country-western dancing, but she'd recently joined them anyhow, and was glad she had. Witnessing the devotion in every look he sent her mom was well worth the boot scoots and grapevines. Most of all, her mother's returning confidence continued to swell Jenna's heart. New jeans that had replaced her mother's stretch pants were a mere bonus.

"How about some lunch to celebrate?" Jenna asked. "I say we show off our new looks."

Her mother fingered her flattened bangs, as if deciding. Then she smiled with a youthful giddiness and nodded. "My treat this time."

Reluctant, Jenna agreed. Until she found a job, and could afford more than her own TV dinners, she wasn't in the position to argue.

"I just need to freshen up first," her mother said.

"I'll meet you in front." Jenna headed to the reception area. While waiting, she glanced out the window. She spied a familiar face in the store across the street.

Could it be . . . ?

Antique stores traditionally ranked as her least favorite hubs. She dreaded the musty air, cramped spaces, and clash of displays. For the potential reward, however, she was willing to endure.

She turned to the receptionist. "Please tell my mom I'll be right back."

At the window display, her nose an inch from the pane, Jenna delighted in her find. Once more, it was the squatty monk. Make that *lots* of squatty monks.

Side by side they stood, like a village of holy men. Varied in size, they wore wreaths of gray hair, brown robes, and rosy cheeks. She scanned the queue with hope. A large water pitcher and gravy boat. Salt and pepper shakers. A sugar cup and . . . there it was! A fully intact creamer, handle and all. It was a perfect replacement for the set inherited from Aunt Lenore. Silly or not, Jenna felt like it completed the memory of the sweet old woman. She couldn't imagine a more meaningful gift for her mother.

If she wanted to keep the surprise, she had to hurry.

A bell on the door jangled as she entered. She prepared for a dusty waft. Instead, the lemony scent of polished wood welcomed her. At the sales counter, she joined the line of two other customers. The cashier's gentle eyes matched his Santa-style beard, and his knit snowman pullover could sweep a national contest. For ugly Christmas sweaters, that is.

Cha-ching, cha-ching.

The antique register, while pretty to look at, wasn't the fastest way to do business.

She tapped her toes, hoping to subliminally rush the guy along. Soon she realized she was keeping time with the tune playing on the speaker. "Jingle Bell Rock" had a pretty catchy beat—

She stopped mid-thought and rolled her eyes. Yet she couldn't help smiling. Aliens must have replaced her grinchlike heart while she slept.

The first customer finished and the line moved up.

Cha-ching, cha-ching.

Tamping her impatience, Jenna glanced around the store. A baby buggy was parked nearby, its oversized wheels weathered from walks. On the maple vanity lay a silver shaving kit, beside it a mother-of-pearl hairbrush. How often had they been used to primp for a special occasion?

As if transformed by a wand, the old, worn items surrounding Jenna became anything but "junk." They were storytellers. Rather than price tags, she now saw their tales. A wedding knife and server had shared a couple's first cake. A jukebox had played records for a patron-filled diner. An army jacket had witnessed triumphs and tragedies. Come to think of it, the chocolate-hued uniform, fit for a woman, was used during World War II.

Topped with a cap, the mannequin enticed Jenna over. She touched the stripes sewn onto the sleeve. Her heart cinched at the thought of Estelle and not seeing the family again. The sale was only two days away.

THE CHRISTMAS COLLECTOR / 97

"She's a beauty, isn't she?" The clerk gestured to the uniform, eliminating the possibility that he was speaking of Estelle. "Hard to find a 'Hobby hat' in such good condition. Are you a fan of memorabilia from World War Two?"

"I guess you could say I've become one."

His face lit up. "Got lots of stuff sprinkled around. More things from the Women's Army Corps, too, if you're interested. Most are priced well below value. People just don't realize what they're worth."

"No," she said sadly, "I bet they don't."

"You know, my mother-in-law served with them over in Europe. Never spoke about it much, though." As he rubbed his beard, Jenna perked.

Was there more to Estelle's secrecy than Tom Redding? The mystery continued to nag at Jenna. She hoped she wasn't prying by asking, "Do you happen to know why she didn't talk about it?"

"Oh, I dunno," he said. "I imagine it wasn't the most acceptable job at the time. Taking care of the kids, having dinner on the table by five—back then, that was the role women were proud of. Or were supposed to be, at any rate."

As a modern woman, independent and career-driven, Jenna hadn't thought of it that way. It seemed almost too simple, and yet made absolute sense.

The man jerked his thumb to the side. "Would you like to see more stuff like this?"

Yes prepared to spill from her mouth when she remembered her mother. "Another day would be great." Jenna would definitely be back. "For now, I'll only need the monk creamer from the front window."

"Oh, sure, sure. Even got the original box for it in the back room. Stay right here."

Jenna watched him scoot off, rounding a table of porcelain dolls. As he reached into the display, her cell phone rang. She expected to see the salon's number, calling on behalf of a concerned mom. To her surprise, again it was Sally.

"Tell me you didn't do it," she demanded, obviously about Jenna's career.

"Afraid so." Jenna would explain her reasons but on another day.

"So what's next?"

"I'm figuring it'll come to me, hopefully sooner rather than later."

The clerk, creamer in hand, pointed toward the back room. Jenna lifted her hand in acknowledgment as he traveled through the store, neatly displayed and packed with enough valuables for a museum.

A museum . . .

A display . . .

Valuables . . .

The idea materialized, a weaving of scattered threads. With all of Jenna's connections to brokers and collectors, why hadn't she thought of it before?

"Hey, Sally. Is the history museum still trying to replace that exhibit? The one that was going to be on Jackie O."

"Um—yeah. Why's that?"

Jenna's excitement simmered. She prayed Terrence hadn't donated that shoebox. "Hold on." She held the phone to her chest and called out to the clerk now emerging from storage, "Sir, how much for the Women's Army Corps items?"

"From World War Two?"

"That's right."

"Depends." He scratched his head. "Which ones?"

Jenna smiled. "All of them."

Chapter 16

Christmas Eve had arrived, and Reece still couldn't decide whether or not to go. In the shadows of his car, parked downtown, he remained a block away. He flipped his key over and over in his hand. According to his mom, the museum had made a point of confirming the family's attendance. A variety of his grandma's estate items had been added to their permanent collection. As a holiday treat, they'd all been invited to the premier showing.

Well, not Reece necessarily. With Jenna Matthews somehow involved, he doubted the invitation was meant for him.

Since parting ways with Tracy, he'd once gotten up the nerve to give Jenna a call. The message he'd left her, a belated thanks for her help at the hospital, felt pathetically transparent. How do you slip into a casual voicemail that you're no longer in a relationship? Answer: you don't.

Not surprisingly she didn't call back.

What a jerk he must have seemed. Reece was probably a major reason she had cut ties to the estate, to prevent crossing paths. By now, she'd surely moved on to another sale and left thoughts of him behind. And yet, the possibility of seeing her again had been powerful enough to draw him here.

Though maybe not to the front door.

He envisioned his family just now walking in: his sister with her husband, his mother and grandma. And his dad. Since their hospital run-in, his breakup with Tracy would have provided even more ammo. The awaiting lecture was as appealing as tonight's show—personal elements of his grandparents' lives, laid out for gawking strangers. Despite the honor of a museum's acquisition, a public display made him uneasy.

Again, Reece flipped over his car key. The ignition slot like a magnet, it urged him to start the engine. He could face his dad in the morning, before the family gathered for Christmas . . . .

Enough. Too often where his dad was concerned, he found himself acting like a kid. Now more than ever, his grandma deserved the family's support. If he'd learned nothing else—from the accident, from her secret past—it was how to put the needs of others first. Tonight he'd act on that lesson.

He straightened the necktie of his suit and exited the car. Within minutes, he was climbing the concrete steps toward the pillared entry.

"Welcome," a woman said at the door. "Your name, please?"

"Reece Porter."

"Ah, yes. The rest of your party's already checked in." She ran a yellow highlighter through his name, listed alphabetically on the sheet. "I hope you enjoy your evening."

So did he.

"Thank you."

Inside, behind a USO banner, three ladies in vintage uniforms stood on a low, miniature stage. They harmonized about yuletide carols being sung by a choir. Red, white, and blue bunting decorated the walls. A waiter with a tray of champagne offered Reece glass. Microbrews were more his style.

"No thanks," he said, a moment before he spotted his dad alone, depositing an armful of jackets at the coat check. "On second thought."

The server handed over a half-filled flute that Reece finished in two gulps. Through a scattering of guests, his father glanced over. The look on his face confirmed he had plenty to say.

Reece set aside his glass and waited, steeling himself. He suddenly wished he'd swallowed his pride and reached out before now, so their confrontation would already be done.

"Reece," his father greeted evenly.

"Dad."

A tense beat passed, the unspoken like shards of ice, clear and sharp.

"So where is everybody?" Reece asked.

"In the other room there." His father gave a nod toward the end of the hall, where murmured discussions drifted out over the tiled floor. Then he peered at Reece and spoke firmly. "I'd like to have a word with you first."

Here it came.

"It's in regard to what you said, about me not supporting you."

"Dad, please. I know where this is going." To have peace in the family, especially at Christmas, Reece was willing to apologize. Certainly there were things he, too, could have handled better.

Yet his father charged on. "I've pondered it a whole lot, and the thing you need to hear is—"

Strangers strolled past, hopefully out of earshot.

"—I've been wrong."

Reece blinked. He reviewed the words, a shock to his senses.

"Fact is, in my line of work, I've been trained to prepare for the worst. And I guess that's made me a little . . . overprotective."

Baffled, Reece continued to stare.

"I hope you can at least see why I acted like I did. After getting that call to come to the hospital . . ." His dad shook his head, trailing off. Color rose in his neck, and his eyes gained a sheen.

No question, for both of them, his grandma's recent collapse had ratcheted up their last confrontation.

"It's okay," Reece offered, barely audible. He cleared the emotion from his throat. "I think we were both on edge, worrying about Grandma."

"No, Reece. I meant when I got the call for *your* trip to the ER."

The second twist again took Reece off guard.

His dad released a breath, hands on his hips. "I know I've been tougher on you since then. But you have to understand, that drive to get there . . ." He finished in a near mumble. "Well, it was about the longest of my life."

Reece had been so terrified over Tracy's condition, he hadn't thought of how strongly his parents, namely his father, had been affected by the scare. How much his father must have always been unnerved by Reece's reckless stunts, for fear of a phone call no parent wanted to receive.

The stress of waiting for word on his grandma's episode had given Reece a taste of that fear. He didn't see until now how alike he and his dad were. Both had been trying so hard to control things they couldn't.

"For what it's worth," Reece admitted, "I've been wrong too. About a lot of things."

After a thoughtful pause, his father nodded. "Guess we're not always as brilliant as we give ourselves credit for."

Reece's mouth curved into a smile. He placed a hand on his dad's shoulder. "Don't worry," he assured him, "I won't tell Mom you said that."

They shared a laugh, slicing through the remnants of tension. Clearly, many more discussions would be needed to strengthen their relationship. But for now, Reece couldn't think of a more promising beginning.

Chapter 17

Almost showtime, but still no sign of him.

A good thing, Jenna reminded herself as she surveyed the reception hall. She needed to stay alert in case of any snags. Families of elderly guests and major donors congregated about her. The ribbon cutting would commence at any minute.

She lifted her posture, savoring the confidence of her burgundy cocktail dress and pumps. Utmost professionalism was essential to her new boss, the director of the private museum. Jenna still couldn't believe her good fortune. She wasn't about to let Reece Porter indirectly ruin it. In his presence, she never failed to revert to a teenager—full of blushes and stammering and being too easily tempted to cross the line of morality.

"They're such nice people," Jenna's mom exclaimed, returning with Doobie, whose western sports coat dressed up his jeans and boots. "That Estelle is just so charming."

"She's definitely an amazing woman," Jenna agreed.

"And Sandy and her daughter, Lisa? Just fabulous."

Jenna had no idea introducing her mom to the three Porter women would have surpassed basic, cordial greetings. Rather, it became a fifteen-minute exchange from which Jenna had to excuse herself, for fear Reece would join them when he arrived.

Skirting the notion, she again admired her mom's black pantsuit, as modern as her hairdo. She'd never looked lovelier, or happier. Granted, a gaudy peacock brooch glimmered from her collar, an accessory that oddly put Jenna at ease. An improved mom was great—not an altogether new one.

"Rita, tell her the news," Doobie encouraged, sweetly touching her chin.

"Oh, yes! I almost forgot." She angled toward Jenna. "Apparently"—an inserted pause to build suspense—"since Sandy's on the auction committee for the Children's Cancer Association, she's going to call me next week about their gala. They're not happy with their photographer, so she wants to talk about working together."

"Mom, that's wonderful."

"I really have Doobie to thank for talking me up, even though *he's* actually the one they should be hiring."

"Ah, bologna," Doobie said. "You're gonna do such a good job, you'll be gettin' calls from all over town. Won't she, Jenna?"

"Absolutely."

Doobie was right. A prestigious event like that had the potential to boost her mother's career, particularly with Sally's support.

"I say we toast to the both of you," he declared. "How 'bout some bubbly?"

The flutters in Jenna's stomach wouldn't mix well with alcohol. "Maybe later."

"I'll take a glass," her mom replied.

"Be back in two shakes." With a wink, Doobie disappeared into the crowd, just as a museum docent approached. She appeared on the verge of panic.

"Jenna, have you seen the big scissors for the ribbon?"

Pressure to impress their patrons, to smooth over the Jackie O mishap, magnified the importance of every detail.

"Last I saw," Jenna said, "they were at the front desk. Bottom drawer."

"Ah, phew. Thank you!"

When the woman sped away, Jenna's mom gazed around the room. She spoke in amazement. "I can't believe you put this together so fast."

"Mom, I didn't exactly do it on my own."

Her mother waved this off and met her eyes. "The point is, I'm very, very proud of you."

Jenna felt a glow inside. She recognized it as a deep, genuine pride, not only for the person she was becoming—more of herself, if that made any sense—but for the mother standing before her.

"Ooh, I almost forgot." Her mom reached into her purse and retrieved a wrapped, palm-sized box. "I brought along your Christmas present."

Jenna hesitated, though not because of a resistance to gift giving this time. The buzz of the teeming space, and weaving of waiters with passed hors d'oeuvres, didn't make the moment ideal. What's more, she'd left her mother's collectible creamer, wrapped with a few other goodies, back at her condo—the home she thankfully wouldn't have to give up.

"Wouldn't it be better if I open this tomorrow?"

"You could, but I thought it might bring you luck for tonight." The sparkle in her mom's eyes made it impossible to decline.

Jenna removed the paper, and out of the rectangular jewelry box she pulled a beautiful silver bracelet made of Cheerio-sized links. A shiny heart, engraved with her initials, dangled from the middle: *For J. M.*

She ran her finger over the letters, fully understanding what she held. A mother's symbol of love. Many decades from now, maybe a stranger would find it in a flea market or an antique mall. And maybe, if fortunate enough, that person would sense its story.

"Thank you," Jenna whispered. "I love it." Tears welling, they traded a long heartfelt hug.

Then stepping back, her mom relieved her of the box and wrapping. "I'll go throw these away for you."

Jenna nodded at the simple but meaningful offer; her mother was now taking care of others. Awed by the change, Jenna again admired her bracelet. She placed it around her wrist and secured the clasp. Luck tonight might come in handy.

"Merry Christmas, Jenna," said a man's voice. She knew that smooth timbre.

Against the weight of dread, she straightened.

Reece Porter. A sleek, charcoal suit and black shirt accentuated the broadness of his shoulders. Given his burgundy tie, a near-perfect match to her dress, a person could easily mistake them for a couple.

"I didn't think you were going to be here." Her greeting inadvertently sounded more hopeful than observant.

His tentative smile lowered as he motioned behind him. "Guess I could catch a movie down the street instead."

"No, I didn't mean—I meant—when I didn't see you with your family, I thought . . ." Once again, he'd made her a flustered mess. "Do you need help finding them?"

"Nah, I already did, thanks. Just wanted to come over and say hi."

"Well, hi." She glanced away, mentally scraping for an excuse to escape. But her mind was too busy scolding her pulse. Why did it insist on quickening at the sight of those dark brown eyes?

"So," he drew out. "How goes life in the estate world?"

The question threw her off. She thought he would have heard the news from Sandy. Although why would he ask about her? He had a gorgeous, raven-haired girlfriend to occupy his thoughts.

"I'm not in the business anymore."

THE CHRISTMAS COLLECTOR / 107

"I didn't realize."

She lifted a shoulder and said pointedly, "Turns out, it wasn't a good fit."

"You find something better?"

Had he missed her message? Or was he challenging her? "I'm working at the museum now, as an assistant with acquisitions."

"Wow," he said. "So life is good, then."

"Life is good." She meant to smirk at him, but his return smile melted the smugness right out of her. Then a question came to mind, a cool splash of water. "Will your girlfriend be joining you tonight?"

At that, his gaze fell away. Thank God. But then he shook his head and said, "We're not together anymore."

"I see."

Wait—*what*?

"I guess you could say we weren't a good fit. Just took us a while to see that."

The echoed sentiment reverberated between them. She tried to resist, but her defenses, flimsy as they were, couldn't compete against his undeniable sincerity. "I'm sorry it didn't work out."

"Actually, it did—is," he amended. "Everything is working out. Just not the way I'd pictured, maybe."

Although cautious, Jenna allowed herself another look in his eyes. In them she found mutual understanding, a commonality of unexpected paths. Whose life ever turned out the way they planned?

"Ladies and gentlemen, your attention, please."

The female voice abruptly reminded Jenna of her surroundings, the task at hand. Her boss, Dee Ann, appeared at the arched entrance of the main hall. A wide red ribbon, tied into a Christmas bow, created a horizontal barricade. Behind her, a closed velvety curtain blocked early peeks.

Jenna projected a look of attentiveness.

Dee Ann raised both arms, palms to the back in an Evita-like pose. The signal worked, and the USO singers concluded their song in a few quick bars. The room fell to a hush. It was all a tad dramatic, but so was Dee Ann. And Jenna liked her that way. During the past two weeks of preparations, Jenna had come to adore the woman and her boundless passion for history.

"We are extremely pleased to have so many esteemed guests with us this evening," Dee Ann resumed, gesticulating. Not the safest of habits with the oversize scissors in her hands. "While we had originally planned to showcase the life of Jacqueline Kennedy Onassis, I firmly believe the collection we've prepared is equally impressive. Maybe more so, as it spotlights significant heroes in our nation's history who all too often go unrecognized."

As Jenna strove to listen, she could feel Reece stealing side glances in her direction. She direly hoped the heat crawling up her neck wasn't betraying her with a beet red hue.

In what seemed a hundred hours later, Dee Ann wrapped up her speech, cut the ribbon, and on cue, two docents slid open the curtains. The crowd murmured as they traveled forward. Over the heads of the herd Jenna located her mother and Doobie. She gestured for them to go on in, that she'd catch up with them soon. Wafts of perfumes and colognes, plenty of Old Spice, mingled in the air.

"Here comes the gang," Reece reported as his family drew closer.

Estelle stood at the helm in an emerald green dress and pearls, her expression distraught. "I really don't see how anything of mine would've been important enough to be here."

"Well," Jenna said, "why don't we find out?"

Estelle eyed her at length, then yielded by shuffling into the stream of people. Jenna followed, batting away doubts that this was a mistake. She again told herself: Once Estelle viewed her achievements in a revered display, and with family at her side, she would fully embrace her due credit.

On the right, they came across the uniform that had kicked all this off. It now hung sleek and pressed on an elegant mannequin. Yellowed wartime letters filled the case to its side.

Estelle paused for only a second before continuing onward.

Military recruitment posters, framed and mounted, zigzagged down the wall. They featured colorful drawings of women in every branch: the WACs and WAVES, WAFS and WASPs, ANCs and SPARS, and more. What began as an idea to honor the members of the Women's Army Corps had expanded to include thousands of others.

Jenna still had trouble keeping all of their acronyms straight, if not her gratitude for what they had sacrificed. She hoped that message was coming through, but Estelle's face remained unreadable.

The rectangular display case awaited on the left. Jenna debated over pointing it out, but then Estelle halted. She squinted behind her glasses while angling her walk. Her Bronze Star, labeled with her name, was propped beside a collage of photos. Though they all featured her unit in the Pacific, only a few of the pictures had belonged to Estelle.

She stood there, staring at the case. Not saying a thing. No smile, no happy surprise. Just a quiver in her hands.

"Toss them out, donate them, do as you'd like."

Those were the words she'd used when Jenna had first presented the keepsakes. Could she have truly meant she wanted them destroyed?

"Mom, are these of you?" Sandy asked, confounded.

Still, nothing in response.

The family closed in on the case, studying the items intently.

Jenna felt the angst of an unprepared symphony conductor. She was orchestrating a performance headed rapidly for disaster.

"How did you . . ." Estelle began in a rasp. Her gaze remained on the pictures. "Where did you find all of these?"

An honest answer might only make things worse.

"Mrs. Porter, if you're not comfortable with this, I could certainly let the director know."

They could remove at least the Porters' belongings—Jenna hoped.

Estelle's ragged breaths suggested she was starting to cry. Jenna moved closer, flashing back to the woman's health scare. But then Estelle glanced up to reveal a growing smile. The puffs of exhales came from quiet laughter, not tears.

"Hard to believe it," she said, motioning downward, "but that's how we did our laundry in a bind."

Moisture from sheer relief sprang to Jenna's eyes. Amid the collage was a photo of Estelle and a stunning light-haired woman. They were wringing out garments over upturned helmets.

Estelle gained a reminiscent tone as she went on. "Gracious, everything we owned molded in that humidity. And the mosquitoes?" She blew out a sigh. "All bigger and deadlier than Sasquatch."

Jenna grinned as Estelle's focus went on to the next picture. Three ladies sat in a Jeep while Estelle leaned against the hood. Palm trees in the background dotted the scene.

"Would you look at that," she said. "Roz . . . and Betty. You know they used to call us the SOS girls, Shirley and me, on account of our names."

"I'd heard that," Jenna replied in truth, then diverted from an inquiry about her secret source. "You must have worked hard to take care of the patients there."

With a calmed hand, Estelle touched the glass, hovering over a snapshot. A WAC was serving a food tray to a bedded soldier. "Met some real good fellas in that ward." Her response carried a current of bittersweet memories. Something in it confirmed that the reference wasn't limited to patients.

Reece's father turned from the collection. "Mom, this is the

Bronze Star," he said, a near whisper. "Why didn't you ever tell us you served in the war?"

When Estelle fumbled for an answer, Reece interjected, "Because she thought her past was something to be ashamed of, when really she ought to be proud."

The warmth and meaning of his words seemed to resonate with his grandma, as well as his father. In fact, they had the same effect on Jenna.

"What a cute dog," Lisa said, viewing the photo of Estelle with a Yorkshire pup.

"Ahh, yeah," Estelle replied. "She used to ride with a flight crew. Called her . . . oh, what was it? Smoky, I think. Her tricks were great for cheering up patients. The staff too." Estelle shook her head with an air of remembering, and asked Jenna, "Wherever did you find these?"

As if summoning the answer, in the most literal sense, Jenna spotted his face. Tom Redding stood across the thinning room, dapper in his bow tie and gray suit. He'd claimed he was too busy to come, a blatant excuse. Yet he had gathered the nerve after all.

"To be honest," Jenna replied, "I had a little help."

Estelle wrinkled her brow. Her gaze proceeded to trace where Jenna had been looking and discovered the elderly gentleman. As he made his way over, he removed his fedora and smoothed his silver hair.

Recognition captured Estelle's face, punctuated by her hand to her lips.

They stood only a few feet apart.

"How are you, Stella?"

Again, she had fallen silent and still.

The tension palpable, Tom tried again, "You're looking lovely."

Reece touched Jenna's elbow. *Who is this?* he mouthed. The rest of his family appeared just as bewildered.

Tears mounted in Estelle's eyes, mixed with questions. Beneath those arose a history of romance and heartbreak. Had Estelle harbored too much of the latter to even return a greeting? Maybe Tom should have mailed the letter he'd mentioned, to test the waters first.

A metal tinkling entered the air. At the end of the room, adjacent to the next hallway, Dee Ann jingled a bell over her head. "Pardon me, everyone. But we have a special performance about to begin in the next hall. If you'll kindly follow me."

The USO girls were scheduled to sing a tribute. Jenna had helped assemble the small stage between the "Rosie the Riveter" area and that of the All American Women's Baseball League. It was a highlight that now mattered little, for Jenna's heart ached for Tom—who angled sideways, as if to leave.

But he didn't. Rather, he was daring to offer his elbow. "Shall we, Stella?"

She glanced down, then back at his face. The whole family was watching, waiting.

After a long beat, she slowly raised her arm and hooked it through his. Although inquiries in her eyes persisted, the smile stretching her lips mirrored the one now lighting Tom's face. Evidently, he had no need for a letter. He'd delivered himself instead.

Together, the couple walked out of the emptying hall. Reece's parents exchanged looks of pleasant interest, and the rest of the family followed behind.

Except for one.

Reece gave Jenna's sleeve a soft tug, turning her around. "You mind filling me in?"

To best explain, she guided him to the last photo. Tom was holding a small branch above Estelle's head. "That's them."

Reece leaned down for a closer view. "What's he got there?"

"Makeshift mistletoe."

He grinned. "Smart guy."

When Reece stood up, the distance to Jenna shrank to inches.

From the warmth of his breath and realization of their being alone, she fought off a shiver. Tenderly, he moved a stray hair from her cheek, where his hand then lingered.

"So, did it work?" he asked.

"What's that?"

"The mistletoe."

She shook her head *no*.

"That's too bad."

Through the fog of Jenna's thoughts came the rest of the story. "After their holiday party, though, she found him behind the supply tent."

"Oh? Then what?"

Before she could answer, he demonstrated a guess by pressing his lips to hers. She hedged for a second, merely from surprise, then wrapped her arms around his neck. She could feel his heart against her chest and lost herself in the beat. His hands rounded her waist and pulled her close. As he kissed her deeper, newness battled the familiar in the taste of his lips, the scent of his skin. The mix of comfort and uncertainty formed a tangle of thoughts. A collection of feelings.

Jenna never wanted it to end.

Dear Reader,

Only upon completing this novella did it occur to me that my literary journey had come full circle. After all, it was a family Christmas gift that had sparked the idea for my debut novel. The fact I had "borrowed" two characters from that story in order to create *The Christmas Collector*, though now as their elderly versions, seems all the more fitting.

You see, I was in the midst of interviewing my grandmother for the biographical section of a homemade cookbook, intended as a Christmas present for the grandkids, when she revealed a shocking detail: She and my grandfather had dated merely twice during WWII before uniting in a marriage that lasted until his passing, fifty years later. Until then, I had no idea their courtship had blossomed almost entirely through heartfelt letters, each of which Grandma Jean then retrieved from her closet to share.

Captivated by their relationship and a fading era, I soon sat down to pen my first novel based on the question: How well can you truly know someone through letters alone? What formed as a result was *Letters from Home*, in which a WWII soldier falls deeply in love through a yearlong letter exchange, unaware that the girl he's writing to isn't the one replying.

True historical accounts continue to fascinate me, particularly those lesser known, which I proudly enjoy highlighting through my stories. Each of them, most recently in *The Ways We Hide*—a World War II tale of a skilled female illusionist recruited by British Military Intelligence MI9 to design escape devices to thwart the Germans, all while evading her own past—shares themes of redemption and forgiveness, loss of innocence, the complexities of family, and the importance of memories. I hope you enjoy *The Christmas Collector* for all these reasons and more!

With warm holiday wishes,
Kristina McMorris

For more about Kristina's books, special book club offerings (including virtual group chats), and even excerpts from the courtship letters by Kristina's grandfather, visit KristinaMcMorris.com.

Gifted

TAMMY GREENWOOD

Sofia

On Christmas Eve morning, Sofia De Luca awoke in her childhood bedroom, and—for a single moment—could have been a child again. Through tired eyes, she spied a kaleidoscope of rosebud sheets and ornate crown molding and a frosty window overlooking the street below, snow swirling outside like bits of glass. And in that soft place between dreaming and waking, she waited for the sound of Ella Fitzgerald's Christmas album, her father's slippers shuffling across the parquet floor, the scents of his coffee and morning cigarette. He only smoked when her mother was gone, but her mother was often gone. Even on Christmas Eve.

In this liminal place of threadbare roses and quiet snow, she allowed herself not only the nostalgia, but the grief of those Christmas Eves past: her mother on tour, her father and she left to fend for themselves. Her mother was a wrapped gift left on the counter along with promises inscribed in her meticulous handwriting: *will miss you, will call, will see you soon.* Despite Sofia's father's efforts (the struffoli wreath from Ferrara's in Little Italy, midnight mass at Cathedral of St. John the Divine,

Christmas stories read aloud by the fire), she longed for her mother. It was an ache that no amount of her father's syrupy Italian hot chocolate could alleviate. But Christmas meant *The Nutcracker* and Handel's *Messiah*, and this meant that her mother, an itinerant classical violinist, was little more than a crackling voice calling from a pay phone and colorful postcards from around the world.

In this in-between moment, she was a child, *that* child. However, as soon as she sat up, she returned to her fifty-four-year-old body, joints aching. She was *here*, now. Her father had passed almost a year ago, and in a strange twist of fate, she had been tasked with caring for her mother—who, while physically present now—was still *absent*.

It had begun with small things: forgetting where she'd put her keys, forgetting why she'd entered a room, forgetting why she'd gone to the store. A fogginess Sofia herself was often troubled by now. But unlike Sofia's absent-mindedness, her mother's illness escalated quickly; soon she was forgetting her own birthday, her address when the cabbie asked, Sofia's name.

Simone had been diagnosed with Alzheimer's when Sofia's father was still alive. But it wasn't until Sofia's father grew sick himself, and it was clear that her mother would outlive him, that she had stepped in to help. Fortunately, Sofia was a caretaker by vocation, if not by nature. She never had children herself, but as a birth doula, she had ushered thousands of babies into the world, caring for them as well as for their mothers in those twilight hours after a baby is born when a mother's changed world comes into sharp focus. It should have been easy, caring for her mother—a grown woman who, despite cognitive difficulties, was (at least for now) able to do many things for herself. But instead of falling naturally into this new role, she'd found herself incapable of the same tenderness and patience she afforded her clients. With her own mother, she was easily irritated. She was trained in massage, but the thought of touching her mother's transparent flesh, of kneading the knots from her narrow back, was repellent. It took every bit of fortitude she could muster to offer the most basic kindnesses: making her breakfast; helping her with her buttons or zippers or laces; steering her back to her room when she woke, delirious, in the kitchen or living room; and once—before she installed the special "dementia door lock"—in the building's foyer by the front door.

Before her father passed, Sofia would come by the apartment two or three times a week, taking the train in from Brooklyn. But after he passed, she'd known she had no choice but to move in. Her mother refused to leave the apartment for an assisted living facility, and because Sofia was unmarried, and not only childless but an only child, this responsibility had fallen squarely on her shoulders.

Her father had, thankfully, ensured that they had the financial resources they needed. His years as a Broadway songwriter meant that in addition to his and Simone's shared savings and his life insurance, she and her mother would continue to receive royalties in perpetuity. Her parents owned the West Village townhouse outright, occupying the second- and third-floor apartment and renting the first-floor flat to a young woman named Lilly. They were able to afford a private nurse, who came by daily as well as whenever Sofia had a birth to attend to. Constance had the precise combination of patience and firmness that kept her mother in line; and oddly, her mother grew softer around Constance. Pliable and childlike. Watching her mother with Constance filled Sofia with a profound feeling she couldn't articulate. Not nostalgia, exactly, but rather a melancholy longing for something, an intimacy maybe, one she and her mother had never shared. Sofia had dated a man from Brazil for a while in her thirties, and he'd said this feeling was called *saudade* in Portuguese. Missing something you never had.

Constance came each morning around nine o'clock. While

Sofia prepared breakfast, Constance was the one to ensure the meal made it into her mother's mouth. Simone was not yet in need of being fed, but she did need some reminding of which utensils to use and occasional coaxing when she insisted she was dieting. Constance was savvy, though—trained in this quiet subterfuge—and within an hour, her mother's plate would be clean. But today was Christmas Eve, and Constance would be with her own family, leaving Sofia and Simone alone to navigate this meal and everything else the holiday held in store.

Sofia raised her arms over her head, which she tilted from side to side, stretching her neck, then looked out the window at the swirling snow falling from a pale sky. It was the kind of snow that melted the moment it touched the ground. *Snow kisses*, her father had called the delicate flakes. The forecast, however, was that it would grow colder and the snow would become heavier. A white Christmas, perhaps.

In the year since she'd moved home, she'd taken to sleeping in her underwear. Her mother insisted on keeping the house a balmy seventy-eight degrees. Some nights, Sofia woke up drenched in sweat, the hot apartment and the raging furnace of her own menopausal body to blame. But now, when she threw off the covers, she was met with an arctic blast of air, raising goose pimples on her skin. The floor was like slabs of ice under bare feet when she stood up.

Scowling, she scurried across the room and threw on a pair of sweats, a fisherman's sweater that had belonged to her father, and slippers. Blowing warm air into her hands, she made her way down the hallway to the living room, where she found the thermostat set, as always, to seventy-eight. Where was the cold air coming from? She glanced around the room, making sure the tall windows were securely shut and locked. She'd affixed dementia locks to the ones that opened to the fire escape as well as on the front door. She doubted her mother would venture out a window, wasn't sure she was strong enough to even open the heavy sash herself, but she didn't want to take any chances.

Shivering, she went to grab a scarf from the hooks by the door and found the source of the blustery air. The hallways in the building were bitter cold this time of year, and the door to the hallway was open.

If their apartment door wasn't latched and locked, and Lilly opened the door to the street downstairs, it would create a vacuum and push their door open. That must be what had happened.

She shut the door and examined the lock, as if it were to blame, but then realized she was likely the one at fault. She'd gotten in at 3:00 a.m. when Dana, the new mother she'd been caring for, finally fell asleep. The husband, Christopher, had sent Sofia home, though she'd offered to stay. "It's Christmas Eve tomorrow," he'd said. "Be with your family." She'd taken a Lyft home and barely made it up the stairs, so exhausted she could hardly see. When she got inside, she'd peeled off her coat and boots, and her phone had started ringing with a FaceTime call. Dana had woken up and was worried about the baby's breathing. "Let me see her," Sofia had said softly as she shut the door. Dana had flipped the camera to the newborn, who was sleeping soundly, cupid's-bow lips sucking at the air. She listened for a moment, heard a faint whistle, and said, "Do you have the suction device I gave you? Use it to clear her nose out; that's all it is."

"Oh, good, thank you. I'll do that," Dana said. "I'm so sorry to bother you."

"No need to apologize. Call me any time."

The midwife had been apologetic; she would be out of town for the next week for the holidays. Sofia had told her not to worry. She would take care of the new little family.

After she hung up with Dana, she'd made her way down the hall and peeked in at her mother, who was fast asleep in a sea of pillows, then went to her own bedroom, where she'd undressed and collapsed.

The door had been unlocked and had blown open. That had to be it, she thought. But even as she was reassuring herself, she was already rushing back down the hall to her mother's room, heat spreading through her chest.

She opened the bedroom door quietly, and felt her knees turn to liquid. The bed was carefully made, pillows fluffed.

Her mother was gone.

Alex

Alex woke to the buzz of a text from her mother. Her pink phone trembled on the nightstand. But when she clicked on the notification, she saw only the most recent of a whole string of texts beginning just after midnight.

Are you home from the theater yet?

How did it go?

Where ARE you? Your locations are turned off. You didn't take the subway home alone, did you? I told you we'd pay for a Lyft.

A missed call notification, followed by another text at 1:30 a.m.:

Oh, phew, the tracker was just glitchy. I see you got home safe. Call when you get up.

Alex was nineteen years old, almost twenty, but her mother treated her as though she were twelve, the way she had the first time she came to the city for a summer intensive at New York Rep. While the other girls lived in a dorm together, her mother had sublet an apartment for them near the studios and had stayed there all six weeks. She walked Alex to class each morning and was there when she emerged from the building at the end of the day. As the other girls went to get dinner or see a movie, she and her mom sat in the stuffy studio apartment eating pre-made salads while she iced her feet and her mom sewed her pointe shoe ribbons and elastics for her.

It wasn't until the summer Alex turned sixteen that she managed to convince her mom to let her live in the dorms with the other girls, but even then, her mom had stayed at an apartment nearby. Just in case. It was mortifying. None of the other girls' mothers were lingering around like this. Luckily, her roommate, Zu-Zu, had only shrugged and said, "She loves you. It's sweet."

Alex had no idea what her mother did all day while she was in classes: window-shopped, maybe? Wandered around the city? When she asked, her mom would grow defensive, saying that she had *plenty* to do. She did do a bit of consulting work, grant writing, mostly. But Alex knew it was her stepfather's income that made all this possible. Her mother's contributions were incidental. *Alex* was her mother's job; her burgeoning ballet career, her mom's occupation.

Alex was an only child. When she was three, her baby brother, William, had died. Her mom put him down for a nap, and he never woke up. Alex didn't remember him at all except for those shadowy memories that were most likely only memories of photos she'd seen (her, pigtailed and small, holding a pudgy newborn on her lap; or the one of his face pressed against her mother's chest), but she often imagined what it would be like if he'd lived. He'd be sixteen now. Driving. He'd have a girlfriend, or a boyfriend. And her mom would have something else to focus on besides Alex and ballet. She wondered if he would have been smart or athletic. Or maybe, God forbid, a dancer, as well. She thought of him often, that almost-brother, about how much she missed what could have been.

At seventeen, she'd been offered a trainee position at the

company, and—miraculously—her mom and dad had agreed that she could room with Zu-Zu in an apartment. They liked Zu-Zu and trusted her. And she was finally out from under her mom's thumb. It's not like she did anything crazy, of course; she was dancing thirty or forty hours a week, too exhausted at the end of each day to do much but collapse on the couch. But at least she had a *life*. After class, she and Zu-Zu would walk home, stopping for coffee or pastries along the way. Ducking into bookstores or bodegas, where they bought themselves bunches of flowers. On Sundays, they lounged around in pajamas all day, watching *Friends*. There were parties, sometimes, with the other dancers. But then Covid hit, and all of it disappeared. That spring, she'd packed up her things and gone home.

Her mother had insisted this was simply a bump in the road, on *her* road, to becoming a professional ballerina. Everyone was in the same boat. Her mother had their garage converted into a makeshift ballet studio, with Marley floors and mirrors and a barre along one wall. She paid for Zoom classes with master teachers from companies all over the world. She made her healthy lunches and snacks every day. That other life in the city began to feel like a dream. All that independence she'd had was gone. The virus had stolen everything. Dancing in a converted garage, hot and sticky in the summer heat despite the industrial fan her dad bought, made her feel claustrophobic. On the worst days, she'd shut the door, turn the video off her Zoom, and just lie on the floor. What was the point of any of this?

"Are you okay?" her mom would ask.

But she had no idea how to explain to her what was going on inside her head and inside her body. How the movements, the combinations, and choreography were like a foreign language to her now.

She thought it might get better when she returned to New York, to her apartment, to the studio. But it persisted. The feeling she could only describe as *joylessness*. When she was ten or eleven, their house had been broken into while they were on vacation. The burglars had stolen the electronics and her mother's best jewelry. From her room, they'd taken the ballerina jewelry box she'd gotten when she was three and had just started ballet. It wasn't valuable, but its absence had upset her. This was how she felt now. As if someone had stolen something irreplaceable.

Her mother must have suspected something was wrong lately, because despite being a three-hour train ride away in Connecticut, she was hovering, the blades of her helicopter propeller sharp and steady and humming. It was even worse than it had been before Covid; her mom was worried all the time now.

How are company classes?
Your Achilles okay?

When Alex had been cast to dance in both "Waltz of the Flowers" *and* "Waltz of the Snowflakes," corps roles with the main company, her mother had been beside herself. **OMG. So proud of you. Aren't you thrilled?**

When she didn't respond:

Alexia. What is going on??

And now this. Alex had no idea how to tell her what had happened last night. Or about how she'd been feeling lately. Because they were tied up together, weren't they?

She squeezed her eyes shut, and tears started to leak, running in two hot streams on either side of her face. When she opened them, she looked out the window, and the swirling snow seemed to be taunting her. The music from "Waltz of the Snowflakes" played in an endless, haunting loop in her head.

She looked across the room at the place where she'd peeled off her tights and left them last night, thinking, despite everything, about how good it had felt. As if she'd just shed her skin. Molting, losing that shell of who she was. But who was she without that pink veneer?

She could hear Zu-Zu in the kitchen; Zu-Zu was always up

earlier than she was. Even on Christmas Eve. And she would want to talk about what happened. She'd want to know what Alex planned to do now, how she could help her fix this. It was a conversation she dreaded almost more than the one she'd need to have with her mom.

Slowly, she crawled out of bed, feeling light-headed as she stood up. She pulled on the ballet pink cashmere robe, an early Christmas gift from her mom, and slid her feet into slippers. She hadn't bothered to wash her makeup off last night, and her hair was crunchy with hairspray. She caught a glimpse of herself in the mirror and didn't know whether to laugh or to cry at the ghoul staring back at her.

In the living room, Zu-Zu was playing the Christmas playlist she'd had on repeat since the day after Thanksgiving. She'd made coffee. The two Santa mugs that her mom, Effie, had sent earlier that month were sitting on the counter. The Christmas tree Zu-Zu's dad had brought all the way from Vermont was aglow with white lights in the window. Underneath were some wrapped gifts sent by both their families. Neither girl would be able to go home for Christmas, not with both Christmas Eve and Christmas Day performances.

"Oh, Lex," Zu-Zu said, reaching her arms out and beckoning her.

Alex felt herself starting to crumble.

"Come," Zu-Zu insisted, and embraced her. Zu-Zu smelled like citrus and honey. She was a human cup of tea: warm and soothing.

Together they stood in the kitchen, as if they were a couple slow-dancing, Zu-Zu holding her, stroking her hair. When she pulled away, Zu-Zu's eyes were filled with tears, too.

"What *happened*?" Zu-Zu asked, her warm brown eyes searching hers for answers she didn't have.

"You saw what happened." The entire audience at the Met had seen what happened.

"I mean, *why*?"

Alex shook her head. She had no words to explain what overtook her last night. About what happened inside her brain. What happened to her body. She didn't know how to explain that the moment the music began, the skittering flutes and fluttering clarinets, she'd left her body. She'd literally felt herself floating upward, a snowflake—weightless. She hadn't felt her feet as they carried her onto the stage. Or off.

Alex shook her head. "My mother is going to kill me."

"Are you going to go talk to Nicholai?" Zu-Zu asked.

"I guess. I don't know what else to do at this point. I really don't have anything to lose."

Zu-Zu handed her a Santa mug. The coffee was steaming hot and smelled of peppermint.

"What will you say?"

Alex imagined walking into Nicholai's office, a place she had been only once before, when he'd offered her the trainee contract. She'd sat in silence that day, awed by the photos on the walls of him dancing with the biggest stars in the ballet world: Wendy Whelan, Alessandra Ferri, Sylvie Guillem. These were the women her mother had idolized, as well, back when she was an aspiring dancer herself. They would have been her contemporaries, if her mother hadn't gotten married. Pregnant. If she hadn't quit.

She felt nauseous thinking about sitting in the uncomfortable chair facing Nicholai's tidy desk as he peered at her over his reading glasses. Judging.

What could she say when he'd made it very clear last night that she was being let go? That her career was over. What could she possibly offer that would change his mind? She knew that she was expendable. They all were. She would be replaced in tonight's performance by some eager upper-level student in the school who had been waiting to pounce.

"I guess I'll just have to see if he'll agree to meet with me," she said. "He might not."

She thought about the way he had looked at her last night. After the performance was over. After she'd emerged from the stage door to find him smoking a cigarette outside. She thought about his dismissiveness. How he didn't even raise his voice. As if what she had done wasn't worthy of his rage.

She sat down on the couch now and watched the snow's dizzying choreography as it fell from the sky. It was Christmas Eve. She was nineteen years old, a ballet dancer in New York City. Her life was supposed to be magical. Electric. But she had, single-handedly, unplugged it. Lights out. End of show.

"Well, you are strong, Lex, and . . ."

"I know, I know," she said, sighing at their private joke. "I can do hard things."

When her phone buzzed, she startled, and the hot coffee sloshed onto her hand.

"Ouch," she said, and Zu-Zu opened the freezer door to grab some ice.

As Alex pressed the ice cube against the pale flesh between her thumb and index finger, she read the text from her mother.

Just got some last-minute tickets to tonight's performance. Surprise! I'll take the train and be there by five. Love you, Sugar Plum.

Sofia

This was not the first time Simone, Sofia's mother, had disappeared.

The first time was this past spring. Sofia had panicked, frantically calling for her, only to find her mother sitting in the tiny backyard chatting with Lilly over a cup of tea at the battered bistro table out there. It was spring, a gorgeous birdsong sort of day, and her mother was wearing a lovely floral sundress and sandals. Simone had been lucid that day, just thoughtless, and Sofia had pleaded with her to please leave a note next time if she decided to leave the apartment.

Lilly, who was in her thirties and lived alone downstairs, had been lovely and compassionate, and had taken Sofia aside after that day and said she would be happy to keep an eye out for her mom. Lilly had lost her grandmother to Alzheimer's and knew how difficult it could be to watch someone you love slip away. Sofia hadn't known how to explain that her mother had slipped away long before Alzheimer's took hold of her; she had been absent most of Sofia's life.

The second time Simone disappeared, it was a sweltering day in the middle of August. There was no note again, but Lilly hadn't seen her this time. After a half hour of walking up and down the block, ducking into every shop and restaurant on Bleecker Street, Sofia had found her mother sitting at a table in an ice cream shop, enjoying a raspberry gelato. Once again, Simone was dressed to the nines, this time in a linen suit and heels, her makeup and hair done. It was summer now, and her mother had thought she was *in Roma*. She'd spoken to Sofia in Italian, inviting her to join her at the *caffè*. Sofia complied, grateful to have found her so close to home, but had felt queasy, unable to eat the dark chocolate gelato her mother had insisted on buying for her.

But today, as she stared down the cold stairwell, she shivered. It was winter now: the city was a minefield of slick sidewalks and steps, never mind the frigid cold. She ducked back into the apartment, went to the kitchen, searching for anything that might reveal where her mother had gone. But there was no note on the counter, nothing written on the whiteboard on the fridge.

Back in the hallway, she checked the coatrack. How strange. Her mother's long down coat was still there. She took a deep breath. She must be in the building. She would never go outside in weather like this without her coat. Simone was confused often, but she never left the house without being appropriately dressed.

Sofia quickly changed into a pair of jeans, slipped on her sneakers, and jogged gingerly down the steep steps to Lilly's door. She rang the doorbell, pressing her ear against the door to confirm that it was ringing, but heard nothing. She waited a few moments and knocked. Again, no sounds coming from inside. Then she remembered: it was Christmas Eve. Lilly's family lived on a farm upstate. She'd said she would be spending Christmas with them, not back until New Year's Eve. She'd asked Sofia if she wouldn't mind bringing in any packages that might be left on the doorstep.

Sofia turned and ran back up the stairs. She rifled through

134 / *Tammy Greenwood*

the coats hanging on the rack, searching to see which one was missing, but found every one of her mother's coats and jackets hanging there. And slung on the last hook was her mother's purse. She unzipped it and looked inside. Keys. Wallet. Phone.

She *must* be here, somewhere.

"Mom?"

They lived mostly on the second floor, but her mother and father had used the open third floor as both office and practice space. Her mother would play her violin, and her father would compose. A thousand times, she'd fallen asleep to the odd symphony of her mother's violin and the clacking of her father's old typewriter. After her father passed, and she'd moved back in, she'd stashed most of her belongings in this attic space, and discouraged her mother from navigating the steep steps up which she now bounded.

"Mom?" she called.

The musty space was dark, just a square of light on the dusty floor made by the large window that faced the street. "Mom?" she called again, as if they were children playing hide-and-seek.

She went to her father's desk, which faced the window, and there it was. The note she'd requested. Her mother's beautiful monogrammed stationery, a single slice of ivory linen. That elegant handwriting she knew so well.

Darling, it read. *I've gone to pick up something special for Christmas. Don't follow me. It's a surprise.*

Damn. She *had* left. Without her coat, to go Christmas shopping.

Yours until the stars fall from the sky, Simone.

This note was not for her. It was for her father, who'd been dead for nearly a year.

Alex

Alex looked at her mother's text in disbelief. Her mother and her stepfather had already come to the city and watched her perform two weeks ago at the beginning of the run. Alex had had a pretty good performance that night, and her mother had been beaming when she met her at the stage door.

"You were *luminous*," her mother had gushed, wiping tears from her eyes as she handed Alex an armful of white roses. Her stepfather had leaned in for one of his trademark awkward hugs. And her youngest stepsister, Callie, who'd come along, mumbled about how pretty everything was.

They'd gone to her favorite Chinese restaurant afterwards, and surprisingly, her mother hadn't blinked when Alex ordered the orange chicken, the deep-fried, battered deliciousness she usually reserved for when her mother was not around. She'd eaten quietly as her mom went on and on about the various dancers, the newly promoted principal who had thrilled the audience as Sugar Plum. "She reminds me of you, Alex. *Someday* that will be you."

Why would her mom come again, and on Christmas Eve?

Her stepbrothers and Callie would be at the house tonight. This had become their tradition over the years: for Larry's kids to come for Christmas Eve, while she spent the night with her dad. Though for the last two years, she'd been in the city performing. Most of her stepsiblings were older, with families of their own. She doubted she'd be missed in the houseful of people. Though maybe her mother wouldn't be missed, either.

Was there any way her mother could know what had happened? But who would have told her? Alex wasn't a student anymore. Nicholai didn't have her mom's contact information, as far as she knew. She was an *adult*.

Not performing tonight, she wrote quickly, heart thundering in her chest.

Three dots as her mother formulated her thoughts. She held her breath.

You said you were cast in Snow tonight. I wrote it on my calendar.

"Your mom?" Zu-Zu asked, sitting down next to her on the couch and leaning against her shoulder to look at the screen.

"What do I tell her?" Alex said.

"I don't know," Zu-Zu said. "Maybe make something up until you talk to Nicholai?"

"She can't come tonight, Zee," Alex said.

I'm injured, she wrote, then realized that this might actually expedite her mother coming to visit. She'd want to swoop in and bring her home. Rest, ice, compress, and elevate her to death.

Oh no. Your Achilles?

No, just turned my ankle. PT says it's fine. But I have to rest tonight. Back to work tomorrow!

Send me a pic? Her mom wrote. **Are they sure it's not a sprain?**

It's fine, Mom. But no show tonight.

For a moment, after she set her phone down, she felt an actual ache in her ankle. A bone-deep pain. But then she realized it wasn't her ankle at all, but her whole body that hurt. She was a bruise.

"What time is company class today?" she asked Zu-Zu.

"Ten. Before the matinee."

"I'll go with you. And try to catch Nicholai after."

"Is this for you?" Zu-Zu asked.

"What do you mean?"

Zu-Zu's eyes were kind and concerned. "I mean, are you going to talk to him because you want to? Or because it's what your mom would want?"

"I don't know," she said. "Probably both."

But that wasn't true at all. During "Waltz of the Snow-flakes," when the haunting female chorus began and the snow started to fall, she'd stopped and stood, as the other girls continued to whirl about her. She'd stood stock-still and stared up into the lights overhead, at the paper snow as it floated down from the battens. Then she'd walked slowly and certainly off stage. But not once, not for a moment, when she broke ranks from her corps, that army of tulle and satin, AWOL in the middle of the performance, did she think of her mother—only about how good it felt to be *free*. It wasn't until she sat in the dressing room, surrounded by the girls who would not speak to her, that she realized that she had made a terrible, terrible mistake.

Sofia

Yours until the stars fall from the sky.

It was the way Sofia's mother signed every letter to her father. Every scribbled missive.

Sofia hadn't thought much about the phrase before. She knew it was from her father's favorite song. The story was that they'd met at a Barbara Lewis show at The Village Gate on Bleecker Street in 1968. Simone had asked him for a cigarette, and he'd asked her to marry him. He'd gotten down on one knee between sets, and sworn he'd love her forever. They were married less than a year later, and would stay married for more than fifty years. Their love story was one for the books, but Sofia had never been able to reconcile it with the two people she knew who spent more time apart than together: her mother gallivanting around the globe, while her father rarely left Manhattan.

Sofia returned to the coatrack, pulled on her dark green puffer, and wrapped a thick scarf around her neck. She started to lock the door behind her but remembered that if her mother came home, she wouldn't have her keys.

Outside, she used a loose brick from the walkway to prop the front door open, though she knew this was essentially an invitation to someone to enter not only the building but their unlocked apartment, as well. She comforted herself with thoughts that it was Christmas Eve, and what kind of monster would rob a house on Christmas Eve?

The steps outside were slick with ice, and snow continued to fall softly as she descended them. She imagined her mother navigating the icy walk and was grateful that she had apparently done so successfully, since there was no evidence of a fall. There was, she realized as she looked at the walkway, no evidence of her mother at all. No footprints in what looked like about a half-inch of snow. How long ago had Simone left?

She walked briskly to the corner, where she ducked into the little Italian market she frequented for Americanos and cannoli. Giuseppe, the old man who owned the shop, liked to flirt with her mother. One morning, when they'd stopped in to pick up some of the homemade burrata her mother loved, her mother had mistaken him for Sofia's dad. Giuseppe had been patient and kind, kissed her hand, and cooed to her in Italian.

The shop smelled of coffee and the yeasty scent of the fresh bread Giuseppe had delivered from his brother's bakery each day. The steaming loaves sat in a basket near the front door.

Giuseppe stood behind the meat counter, slicing prosciutto into pale, nearly transparent slivers. Her mouth watered at the salty, nutty scent.

"Good morning, Giuseppe," she said, and he turned to see her, his serious face warming with a smile.

"*Buongiorno,* Sofia," he said, wiping his hands on his clean white apron.

"Have you seen my mother this morning?"

"Yes, yes," he said.

"Oh," she said, surprised. She hadn't thought it would be

this easy. Her eyes inexplicably filled with tears. "Did she happen to tell you where she was going?"

"She said she had to meet someone."

"*Meet* someone?" she said, remembering the note. Simone had written that she was picking up a special Christmas gift. Had she forgotten this by the time she got to Giuseppe's? "Did she say who?"

"No, I am sorry. She said she was in a hurry. I made her *un caffè*, and she left."

"Do you remember what time that was?" The clock behind the counter read 8:00 a.m.

"She was here, waiting outside for me to open, when I arrived," he said. "Six a.m.?"

Two hours ago. She could be anywhere by now.

"You are worried," he said, coming out from behind the counter. His face was old and kind, his skin freckled with liver spots. His narrow shoulders stooped.

"I am. She didn't even bring a coat."

He tilted his head. "Oh no, no. She was wearing a coat," he said.

"She was?"

"Yes. I remember, because I told her how beautiful it was. I told her she could be mistaken for her lovely daughter in that coat. With the roses? *Bellissima*."

Sofia's coat. Of course, she hadn't checked to see if one of her own coats was missing from the rack. She was glad her mother wasn't out in this weather without a jacket, but she felt troubled. The black velvet duster was one that her mother hated, thought garish. Sofia had bought it ages ago, a thrift-store find from the '60s with toggles and embroidered roses and fur along the collar and cuffs. The idea of her mother choosing this particular coat signaled that she had definitely not been herself when she took off this morning.

"Did she say anything at all about where she was meeting this person?" she asked.

"No," he said. "I am sorry." He walked across the wooden floor to the front counter where the espresso maker sat, a gleaming, steaming beast. "I will make you an Americano," he said. "It is cold out there."

"No, *grazie*. I really need to find her. If she comes back, can you please tell her to come home? The door is unlocked." She added, "Tell her I'm worried about her."

"*Si, si*," he said, nodding before smiling a little sadly "And *Buon Natale*, Sofia."

"Merry Christmas," she returned. *Christmas Eve*. Where could her mother be? Whom did she think she was meeting? Her father? Her throat felt thick at the thought of her father. What would he do if he were here?

Her phone buzzed in her pocket, and she pulled it out, stupidly thinking it might be her mother, letting her know she'd gotten home safely.

So sorry to bother you. But I'm still kind of worried about the sound of her breathing?

Dana again.

No apologies! I have a bit of a family emergency, but I'll check in again in an hour or so. But if she's having any difficulty breathing at all, call 9-1-1 or take her to the ER.

"Oh! Sofia?" Giuseppe said as she opened the door to the swirling snow outside, the electronic bells ringing out sharply at her departure.

She turned to him.

"I almost forgot," he said, wagging one arthritic finger. "She had a suitcase. A small suitcase."

Alex

Alex thought about the last time she'd had to pack up and go home, back when the world shut down. The idea of dragging her suitcase out and filling it with—what?—made her head ache. If not leotards and tights and pointe shoes, then what? What do you pack when you've sabotaged your career?

She knelt and looked under the bed, spying the boot she'd had to wear for five weeks last year when she hurt her Achilles. She thought of the lie she had told her mother and had an idea, though every inch of her knew it was wrong. But really, who was she lately but someone who made bad choices?

She quickly got dressed and, sitting on her bed, pulled on the boot, strapping the Velcro tightly around her imaginary injury. She studied her foot, enclosed in plastic. Could this plan actually work?

Zu-Zu stood in the doorway watching her.

"What are you doing?" she asked.

Shame flushed her cheeks. "I was thinking I could tell Nicholai I turned my ankle last night. That I freaked out, and that's why I walked off stage."

"Oh," Zu-Zu said. No judgment. Only surprise.

"I know, it's a dumb idea," she said. And it was, a dumb, dumb idea. Nicholai would demand she go to see the company's PT, that she go to urgent care. And when the boot came off, a perfectly healthy ankle would be revealed. No swelling. No breaks to illuminate in an X-ray. "What else can I say to him?"

Zu-Zu shrugged. "Why don't you tell him the truth?"

"What do you mean?" Alex said. What *was* the truth?

"About why you walked off stage."

Alex fiddled with the Velcro strap.

Zu-Zu came into the room and sat down in the chair at Alex's desk.

"What *happened* out there exactly?" Zu-Zu asked gently. "Did you forget the choreography?"

Alex shook her head. God, if only it had been that simple. But that wasn't what happened. She remembered staring up into the bright stage lights, watching the first flakes of paper snow fluttering down, and how her body stilled.

"I was remembering this time when I was in elementary school. When I was like nine or ten?"

Zu-Zu waited.

"It was the first Christmas after my parents split up, and I was at my dad's. It was winter break at school. I wanted to spend the whole two-week break with him, but Mom had signed me up for a winter ballet camp at my old studio, so I was only going to get a few days.

"He lives on ten acres, and his house is up on this huge hill. For Christmas that year, he bought me a sled and promised we'd go sledding if it snowed."

Her dad had been so excited to have her at his house; he'd bought all her favorite food. He'd painted her room her favorite turquoise color and let her pick out the matching sheets and comforter. He'd told her that they could do whatever she liked: watch the movies she wanted to watch, go to the places she wanted to go. She told him that all she wanted was for it to snow.

But as each day went by, the forecast remained the same. Cold and dry. Everything brittle, but not a bit of snow.

The day before she was supposed to go back home, the sky became ominous. Heavy with clouds. The temperature warmed. And, as the sun set, the snow started to fall. Her father had made them homemade pizzas: pepperoni and pineapple and basil, her favorite, and they'd rented *Mean Girls*.

"It's snowing!" she'd exclaimed, looking out the window at the snowflakes, scattered across an indigo sky. "Can we go sledding now?" she'd pleaded.

"Oh, honey, there's not enough on the ground to go yet," he'd said. "Maybe by morning?"

But in the morning, her mother was arriving to bring her back home. The next day, she'd start her ballet camp. She'd been dancing for five years already at this point, and she knew her teacher was pleased with her progress. She and her mother had had several hushed conversations in the green room at her ballet studio. And there had been a few conversations about her starting to take private lessons. There had also been a discussion about her mother homeschooling her, so that she could have a more flexible schedule, one that centered around ballet. This ballet camp was important, she knew, because it was being taught by a teacher from the Jacqueline Kennedy Onassis School at American Ballet Theatre in New York City. Her mother said that when she was a dancer, this woman had been her idol. She'd even gotten a pair of pointe shoes signed by her as a gift from her own mother.

But the longing she felt for that snow, for the feeling of the sled taking off down that enormous hill, was deep.

They'd watched *Mean Girls*, but, dejected, she'd crawled into her turquoise bed in her turquoise room and fallen asleep.

When her father woke her up, the digital clock on her nightstand said 3:00 a.m. At first, she'd worried something terrible had happened. That there had been an accident. A fire. But her father had simply ushered her out of bed and had her follow him downstairs, still in her pajamas. In the cold mudroom off the kitchen, he'd coaxed her into a pair of ski pants and a parka, right over her pajamas, as she rubbed the sleep from her eyes. She pulled on her boots and followed him outside.

The clouds from earlier hung heavy in the sky, but with a bright moon behind them, the sky was a ghostly white. And it was snowing. Big, puffy flakes of snow.

He grabbed the sled he'd bought her and a dented silver flying saucer he said he'd had since he was a kid. And together they walked to the front of the house and looked down the steep, snow-covered hill it was perched on.

The first flight down was exhilarating but scary. She'd pleaded with her father to ride with her in the sled, and so she sat in his lap as he pushed off and steered them away from trees and the frozen pond at the bottom. She'd been a chatterbox the whole way back up the hill, saying that next time she wanted to go alone. And she did, flying down the hill, the snow and wind pricking at her cheeks as she flew. The third time, she'd decided to lie flat on her back and look up at the constellations of falling snow as her body became weightless.

In just a few hours, she'd be in the back seat of her mother's station wagon, *The Nutcracker Suite* blasting on the car radio, her mother yammering on and on about how the ABT version didn't have a Sugar Plum Fairy anymore—with only a young Clara and an adult Clara. And how she remembered watching the ABT performance on TV, when she was just a little girl herself. With Baryshnikov and Gelsey Kirkland. The next day, she'd bring Alex to the studio after a battle to get her hair into a perfect bun. There'd be dried fruit and nuts in her purse for breaks. And more whispered conversations between her mother and the teacher, while she pretended she wasn't trying to hear what they were saying.

But now, in this moment, there was only the hush of the snow and the thrill of the flight. She was breathless, weightless; she was nobody—no *body*—at all.

Sofia

A *suitcase*? So, Sofia's mother had somehow gone from believing she was out Christmas shopping for her dead father, to thinking she was "meeting" someone, to packing luggage for some kind of trip?

Fortunately, her mother's purse was sitting at home. While her not having an ID made Sofia feel a prick of dread, without money, her mother wouldn't be traveling—nowhere that required a ticket, anyway. She probably wouldn't be able to board a subway and definitely not call an Uber without someone's help. And while she might be able to hail a taxi, she wouldn't be able to pay for the ride.

She remembered reading once that when a child is lost, the search area is directly proportional to the child's age and the amount of time they had been missing: a young child on foot would only be able to travel a certain distance (in direct proportion to how long they had been gone and the type of environment they were in). There were times lately, she had thought more than once, that her mother was very much like a child. She hoped that this was the case right now. This, in addition to the fact that Manhattan was an island, brought her a small comfort. There was, literally, only so far she could go on foot. And unlike the mother of a toddler, she suspected that any bad actors out there would have little interest in an eighty-year-old woman with dementia and without a purse.

But what if she *was* in danger? Simone hadn't wandered off the family farm. There were so many other things that could go awry in the city. A fall. Walking against the light into oncoming traffic. Sofia looked out the window again at the falling snow. The forecast had said that it would snow most of the day, but that plummeting temperatures after sunset could make it too cold for snow. And too cold for an old woman in an old coat to survive. And no ID. No money. No memory of who she was now.

No. She needed to stop herself from traveling down the familiar path of worst-case scenarios. As a child, she had worked herself into a tizzy every time her mother was gone: envisioning plane crashes and car accidents and terrorist bombings. One thing her job as a birth doula had taught her was that she needed to focus on getting through each moment. The second you began to speculate about all the ways things could go wrong, was the second that you became useless to the mother. To the baby. The midwife or doctor was there to anticipate, to fend off any potential disasters. Her job was to be in the moment, with the mother, to help her navigate her fear and pain. It was best, in most scenarios, to be as systematic as possible. To be aware of the dangers, but to focus on tackling each problem as it presented itself.

She thought about the clues she had about her mother's whereabouts: Christmas shopping, meeting someone, a suitcase. She recited these three things to herself as if they were a mantra. She tried to conjure the image of her mother, wearing that vintage coat and carrying a suitcase, leaving the house on a simple mission to purchase a gift for Sofia's father. Where would she go?

Oddly, this recalled an old memory. A memory of a memory; it felt so far away.

The trip to Italy. Her mother was playing at La Scala in Milan for the ballet's *Nutcracker*. Her father's family was from Milan: her great-grandmother and uncles and cousins. They never took family vacations, but this was an opportunity they couldn't pass up. Sofia's parents had arranged with her school for her to be gone for three whole weeks in January; she'd gotten a homework packet from each teacher. Her mother had balked at the idea, but her father had insisted that it was important she keep up. She'd been in seventh grade back then, middle school. At twelve, she'd gone, overnight, from being a little girl to a demi-woman. Breasts and hips emerging. Her body had felt foreign to her. At school, boys started snapping her bra strap as she walked down the hall. She'd catch them whispering, watching. She knew some of her friends would die for this kind of attention, but it had made her skin crawl. She'd been excited for Italy, if for no other reason than it meant she wouldn't have to go back into the lion's den of public middle school. But when they'd gotten to Milan, she'd found herself even more self-conscious. The Italian boys her age in her great-grandmother's neighborhood had been just as bad as the boys at school, and more vocal about it. But the worst thing was she couldn't understand what they were saying to her.

One afternoon, they'd been out on a walk. Just a few streets away from her grandmother's front door, a group of boys were playing a game with a ball. When they began to cluck and cat-call, her mother had stopped dead in her tracks, held Sofia's hand, and turned to face the boys. She let loose a string of Italian words that made the boys' faces redden, and they scurried away, like the roaches that sometimes appeared in their apartment—scattering when the lights came on. Her mother had sighed and said, "Men are terrible all over the world. If you get married, you marry a man like your father. Do not accept anything less."

For some reason, those words had stuck with her, though she forgot the details of that day. Was her father there, too, straggling behind, looking into the shop windows, whistling an oblivious tune? What she remembered was twofold: first, that her mother had known exactly how uncomfortable those boys were making her, and second, that when she'd given her bit of wisdom, her wide blue eyes had been glossy with tears. Sofia hadn't understood it in the moment, but she now knew that it was a swell of emotion Simone had for her father.

Darling, she had written only hours ago. *Yours until the stars fall from the sky.*

Clearly, her leaving today was about her father. But her father was dead. This meant that she was not lucid. She was not having a "good day" in which the present was clear and certain. She'd woken this morning and left the house on a fool's errand.

And the more time that passed, that circle of possibility widened. With every passing moment, the likelihood of finding her mother wandering the Village grew less and less.

She needed to go to the police. As angry as she knew her mother would be to be tracked down, Simone was clearly in the throes of her illness. Sofia had gotten silver alerts on her own phone before and always felt a twinge of sympathy for those families of missing men and women. Confused and wandering. Yes, her mother would be livid to be lumped in with this geriatric crowd, but what choice did she have?

Standing in front of Bleecker Street Pizza, she quickly Googled to see how close the police station was and counted herself lucky that she had no idea where it was, because in her entire life in the city, she'd never *needed* to know.

Fortunately, the 6th Precinct was only a quarter mile from where she stood, the rich scent of the homemade pizza making her stomach growl. She hadn't eaten since last night, when she'd found a granola bar in the depths of her bag during her client's labor.

She started walking up Bleecker Street, grateful for her puffer coat, which was warm, like wearing a down comforter. She thought about the coat her mother had borrowed, the vintage velvet duster, more a fashion statement than a functional piece of winter wear. She hoped she had gotten dressed and wasn't wearing one of those thin cotton nightgowns she wore because the apartment was so damned hot. She shivered at the thought and pulled her scarf more tightly around her neck.

She hurried up Bleecker Street, passing the fortune teller's shop on the corner; the shoe repair shop, where her father brought his favorite loafers whenever the soles wore out; the Village Apothecary, where she filled her mother's prescriptions. Finally, she turned down the tree-lined West 10th Street, and there it was, the police station.

A gust of wind whipped across her face as she stepped toward the door, the blue emblem painted on the building bringing little comfort. But what else did she have? Her father was gone. She had no family. This was her mission alone.

Alex

While Zu-Zu took a shower, getting ready for company class, Alex sat at their table, drinking coffee from the Santa mug. She knew she shouldn't drink too much; caffeine made her jittery. Usually, she started each day with a green smoothie her mom used to make for her: kale, spinach, protein powder, and pears. Her Christmas gift last year had been a powerful blender that would liquify any fruit or vegetable you could think of. The blender sat on the counter now, and she had the illogical feeling that it was judging her.

Her mom told her that when she was a dancer, there hadn't been any focus on health (physical or mental) for dancers. The only goal had been to be thin. At any cost. She told horror stories of her classmates sucking on Tic Tacs instead of eating lunch. Of cigarettes to squash hunger pains and laxatives to empty the body. Her mom said everyone had an eating disorder back then. Of course, ballet was still messed up. And over the years, Alex knew plenty of girls who starved themselves or binged and purged. But there was more of a focus on nutrition and wellness than there had been back in the 1980s, when her mom was dancing.

There were few photos of her mom from those years. A single black-and-white headshot. A couple of pictures of her in costume, posing. There were no videos at all. Alex had dug through her mom's old photo albums one time when they were cleaning out their garage and had found a single photo of a bunch of girls standing outside, wearing their tights and fluttery skirts. They all held cigarettes, the smoke curling into the air around them like the mist around the dancers in *Swan Lake*. She recognized her mom right away: her face so similar to Alex's own. Big brown eyes, freckles across her nose. But her mother had looked uncomfortable in that picture. Taller than the other girls, self-conscious, cigarette in one hand, the other clasping the elbow of an arm crossed over her ample chest.

Alex knew girls like this. The ones whose bodies suddenly, even violently, defied them. Over the years, they would slowly disappear from the studio. Some when puberty hit. Others as boys started to take interest in those bodies. Others after dipping their toes into the pre-professional world. Companies liked to present the idea that they were amenable to diversity — of ethnicity, or body — but it wasn't true, not in the end. There were limits. Unspoken but real. It took one look at the roster of principal dancers at any company to see that the ones who rose to the top all looked like her. She'd known at least a half-dozen girls who came all the way to the city only to flee after it became clear that they would never be accepted. Some of the old-school ballet masters hadn't gotten the memo that it wasn't appropriate anymore to comment on weight and would pinch the girls' waists or bottoms, grumbling as they did.

Her mother had said at least a hundred times that Alex was one of the lucky ones. After she'd made it through puberty without any major changes, her mother relaxed, as if she'd been holding her breath, waiting for Alex's body to fail her in the way her own had. But she'd insisted that you didn't take this kind of luck for granted. Alex was obligated to take care of this body—one that, her mom argued, had been *designed* as if solely for this purpose. Her mother had always made her feel as if it were her *duty* to dance. And entertaining any other ideas about where her life might go was not only foolish, but *ungrateful*. But to whom was she obligated? Her mother? Herself? What Alex heard, laced through those words, was her mother's fear. That Alex's body, like her own, could still fail her. That no matter how hard she worked in the studio, no matter how many hours she spent at the barre, that her genetics were a ticking time bomb, and that her hips and breasts might one day explode. A woman's body was a dangerous thing, her mother seemed to suggest.

She took another sip of coffee, gone cold now. Normally, she would have had a bowl of yogurt and fruit for breakfast, along with the smoothie. She would have packed a granola bar in her bag. But her appetite was gone, her belly as tight as a wound spring.

She could hear the water running in the shower, and steam escaped through the crack at the bottom of the door. She could hear Zu-Zu humming the Sugar Plum Fairy variation. She wished she could be like Zu-Zu, so in love with dance, in love with this life. Zu-Zu, to whom nothing came as easily as it did to Alex. Zu-Zu, who had had to work extra hard, one of the only brown faces in a sea of whiteness. She envied that for Zu-Zu, ballet was joy, while for her, it felt like an obligation.

She set the coffee mug down, Santa seeming to smirk at her.

She thought again about feigning an injury. She could just put on the boot and go to Nicholai, apologize, plead for him to give her another chance. Explain that she'd twisted her ankle during the first *sauté arabesque*, that the shock of it had stunned her. That it was the first time she'd been injured on-stage and didn't know what to do. She would promise that she would never, ever walk off the stage again.

Yes. A little white lie. And it was Christmas Eve; maybe he would feel sorry for her. Give her the gift of a second chance. She could tell him that she would see her doctor at home in Connecticut while on break. But when she went home, she'd remove the boot and explain to her mother that it had been nothing at all. Because it *had* been nothing at all.

Her gut twisted at the web she was considering spinning. But what was the alternative?

Nicholai had been furious, but calm.

"It is over," he had said to her. "It is a shame. A waste."

When his words returned to her, she felt her heart splinter. And she'd immediately thought of what her mother would think. If she had been there, she would have agreed.

When Zu-Zu emerged from the bathroom, she was dressed in her leotard and warm-ups, a cream-colored full-length romper her mother had knit for her. She looked like a delicate snowflake.

When Alex looked at the boot on her foot and adjusted the straps, she could feel Zu-Zu's eyes on her. But she didn't want to see her expression. She couldn't take her disappointment or her pity or whatever it was she was certain to reveal.

"Are you sure?" Zu-Zu asked.

She looked up, and saw it was pity. Definitely pity.

"I really don't have a choice, do I?" she said.

Their apartment was in Midtown, a straight shot on the 1 Train to Lincoln Center, but they had to walk three blocks to the subway station, and she hobbled along in her boot, pretending that it was, indeed, her foot that was broken, rather than her heart.

They stopped at the bodega on the corner for Zu-Zu to get the ten-cent peppermint patties she loved. She had a sweet tooth but only allowed herself this one little indulgence each day.

"You want one?" Zu-Zu asked as she fished one out of the plastic fishbowl on the counter.

Alex shook her head.

The streets were quiet, the snow falling softly around them. It was Christmas Eve, after all. The rest of the world was home with their families. She could hardly remember the last time she'd spent Christmas Eve anywhere but in the theater.

The subway was practically empty except for an old man, who was reading a newspaper. He looked up as they got on. "Ah, look at these beautiful ballerinas," he said. Zu-Zu smiled, but Alex grimaced. How was it that with a single glance, a perfect stranger could know exactly who she was? *What* she was? She wasn't even in ballet clothes today.

They sat quietly during the ride; the nice thing about being with Zu-Zu was that you could just be quiet. Zu-Zu had her earbuds in—probably listening to the "Snow" music, her hands marking the ghostly choreography.

Alex looked at her phone, though the service underground was spotty.

When they emerged from the steep stairwell at the 66th Street—Lincoln Center Station—her phone came to life. Texts from her mother. Missed calls. Zu-Zu's phone started buzzing, as well.

An alert.

MISSING VULNERABLE ADULT. SIMONE DE LUCA, 80-YEAR-OLD FEMALE, 5' 5", 115 POUNDS, BLUE EYES, CAUCASIAN. SUFFERS FROM DEMENTIA. WEARING BLACK COAT WITH RED FLOWERS.

"Oh, this is sad," Zu-Zu said as she studied the alert on her own phone.

Alex nodded, and the lump that had been in her chest all morning rose to her throat. As she looked at the woman in the photo, her clear blue eyes and confident smile, she thought about how easy it was to lose your way, to forget why you were here. How easy it was to find yourself lost.

Sofia

The woman at the police station assured her that they would find her mother. She took Sofia's information, and within ten minutes or so, her phone dinged with the alert. She thought of her mother's phone, sitting at home on the dining room table, buzzing with the news of her disappearance. She thought how odd it would be if, perhaps, her mother had already found her way home, only to be notified that she was missing. Would she laugh? Or would she be mortified? It bothered Sofia that she really didn't know how her mother would react.

"What should I do now?" she asked the woman at the reception area. She was younger than Sofia, in her thirties or forties, and severe-looking: sharp jaw, pointy nose, and squinty eyes. But she had been patient and kind.

"The alert has gone out. The info will be dispatched to NYPD, as well as to the general public. Someone should spot her soon. We've got your number, and we'll reach out as soon as we locate her."

Despite the chill outside, the air inside the station, like their apartment, was stifling.

"Should I just go home?" she asked, though the moment she said this, she knew that sitting at home while her mother wandered around in the cold was not an option. She needed to be searching, too.

"People are creatures of habit," the woman said wisely. "Even people who are suffering from dementia. *Especially* people who are suffering from dementia. They're almost always found in places that are familiar to them. Part of their routine. They get turned around, or lost in time, but ninety-nine percent of the time, they're located in a place that—somehow—makes sense to them."

Sofia nodded.

"Try not to worry. We'll have her home to you for Christmas. I have a good feeling about this."

"Thank you for your help," Sofia said, realizing she couldn't keep standing there in the police station all day. "I appreciate it. I guess I'll keep looking and wait to hear from you."

"Yes. And please give us a call if you find her, so we can cancel the alert. Merry Christmas."

"Merry Christmas," she said. She glanced up at the clock and saw that over an hour had passed since she'd left home. She thought about that circle widening. About how far her mother could stray. And she remembered the baby.

Shoot.

She texted Dana, **Just checking in. Sorry—still dealing with a family emergency. Please let me know if you need me.**

She waited. No response.

She hoped this meant that Dana was resting. That perhaps, after feeding the baby, they'd both fallen asleep.

She would check in again in another hour. She had told them to call 911 if the baby was struggling at all. And she was almost certain that the baby was just congested. It was incredible how stuffy those little noses could get. And how loud the sounds those stuffy noises made could be.

She wrapped her scarf tightly around her neck and exited onto West 10th Street.

Creature of habit, she thought. But what *were* her mother's habits? Since Sofia had moved home, she'd been surprised by how small her mother's world had become. When Sofia was growing up, her mother was always moving. About the city. Around the world. Their apartment had merely been a pit stop for her: a place to rest up, gather clothes appropriate for her next trip, to retreat to her attic room to practice. But now, she didn't travel anymore. She didn't even play anymore. And her days were predictable: breakfast (half a grapefruit and bowl of steel-cut oatmeal drizzled with honey); a visit from Constance, who oversaw breakfast and medications and hygiene. Simone would listen to music and do the crossword, then read until it was time for lunch. After lunch, she often wanted to go for a walk, and if Sofia wasn't working, she and her mother would walk around the neighborhood. They'd stop to see Giuseppe and pick up something to put together for dinner. On good days, they might walk to Three Lives to browse the books and, purchases in hand, they'd go to Washington Square Park. Here, her mother would contentedly read for an hour or more. They never talked much on these outings. Really, when Sofia thought about it, they were virtual strangers. They always had been.

Maybe she should check the park, she thought. The bookstore. Perhaps her mother was only sitting on a bench, absorbed in a collection of poetry or a new novel. But these were new habits, not old ones. This was the routine of someone who had never had a routine before.

She headed back down Bleecker Street, thinking she'd take the same route that she and her mother would take to the bookstore. When she got to the corner of Bleecker and 7th, she saw the fortune teller's shop and paused.

What harm could it do? she thought. The entire city was

looking for her mother. Perhaps she could get some guidance before she started her own search in earnest.

The front window was shrouded in heavy velvet curtains, only a sliver of the interior visible: an ornate wooden chair, a table, a Tiffany lamp. The glass was painted with gold lettering: PAST. PRESENT. FUTURE.

Present. This was what she needed. She needed to know exactly where her mother was *right now*.

She took a deep breath and tried to open the door. Locked.

Of course; it was Christmas Eve. Most businesses would be closed today.

It had been a crazy impulse, anyway; she wasn't sure what she had been thinking. She turned to keep walking, when she heard someone call out from behind her. "Ma'am?"

She turned around, patting her pockets, thinking she must have dropped something, and saw an elderly woman standing in the open doorway of the psychic's shop.

"Oh," she said.

"I'm sorry," the woman said. "I'm open! I was in the bathroom."

The woman wasn't dressed in fortune teller garb. No turban, no colorful skirts or scarves, no hoop earrings or jangly bracelets. She looked like someone's grandmother. A bright green-and-red Christmas sweater, black slacks, orthopedic shoes. She had neatly trimmed gray hair and a blinking necklace of Christmas lights around her neck.

"Please," she said, waving to her. "Come inside."

Sofia hesitated but obeyed, entering the shop after the woman, who waddled toward the table Sofia had spied through the window. The woman sat in one chair, and Sofia sat in the one opposite her.

The table was spread with a purple cloth, and in the center was a silver pouch.

"I can read your cards," the woman said, pointing her chin to the pouch. "Or your palm. Or we can just chat."

Sofia shrugged. She'd never been to a psychic before.

"Do you want to tell me why you are here?" the woman asked.

Shouldn't she know that? Sofia wondered.

"You have lost someone," she said.

Pretty good guess, though most people had lost someone. Sofia had lost many people in one way or another: her father, partners, and now her mother.

"Yes," she offered, but did not elaborate.

The air was suddenly thick with a familiar smell, the same perfume her mother wore. Her mother had worn this scent since Sofia was a little girl. Often, when Simone came home from one of her trips, she would know her mother was back simply by the smell of the air. She hadn't met anyone else who wore it before.

"Is that One Thousand?" she asked. "Jean Patou?"

The woman cocked her head curiously.

"Your perfume," she clarified.

"I don't wear fragrances," she said, crinkling her nose. "Allergies."

"Oh," Sofia said.

Still, she swore she smelled the heady floral scent. Her mother had bought her first bottle at a *parfumerie* in Paris. And when Sofia was twelve years old, Simone had taken her to Bigelow's Pharmacy in the Village and told her that it was important that every woman have a special scent that belongs to her. For nearly an hour, her mother had patiently waited as she dabbed various perfumes onto her wrists, trying to choose. Sofia had left with another French perfume, Anaïs Anaïs, in a pretty white porcelain bottle. Funny, she hadn't thought of that afternoon in forever, but she still wore Anaïs Anaïs, a scent which she thought of as her own.

"Here," the woman said. "Let me read your palm. I will help you find her."

"Who?" she asked. Lucky guess—she had a fifty-fifty chance of getting the gender right.

"The one you lost."

Sofia extended her hand and wondered how this woman, in her ugly Christmas sweater, would find her mother in her own palm.

Alex

"Alexia," Nicholai said.

Alex sat across from him at his desk in his office. Once again, she gazed at the familiar black-and-white photos documenting his illustrious career, the leather-bound books on the shelf, his blotter filled with scribbles and the chaos of *Nutcracker* season's schedule. He was a busy man, but he had made time for her. For whatever reason, he'd agreed to speak to her.

She had waited in the wings while the company took class onstage. Her favorite ballet mistress, Nicholai's wife, Ulyana, was leading class, and she watched the familiar gentle way Ulyana eased the dancers' bones and muscles and breath into motion. Alex had closed her eyes and listened to the soothing sound of slippered feet doing *tendus* and *rond de jambs*. The crinkly sound of trash bag warm-ups and the cracking of joints as the men and women *pliéd*. Ulyana wove between the bars, correcting and directing the combinations. She was so much kinder than the other rehearsal directors, more mentor than drill sergeant.

Maybe she should have spoken to Ulyana first; maybe

Ulyana could have persuaded her husband that he'd made a mistake in firing her. But it was too late now. Ulyana had seen her in the wings. Eyebrows raised, she had looked at Alex's boot and pressed her hand to her heart in a sad gesture of compassion. And what were her other options? How could she possibly explain what had happened out there? She hardly understood it herself.

After class, Nicholai had appeared onstage to go over notes for that afternoon's performance. When he saw her standing in the wings, he also had looked at her boot, then at her face. She'd felt like he had X-ray vision, able to see that her foot was perfectly fine inside that boot.

"May I speak to you?" she asked softly. "To explain?"

He had agreed, offered her five minutes, and now, she sat with the boot affixed to her foot, feeling overwhelmingly guilty. This ruse was beginning to seem like less and less of a good idea.

She needed Nicholai to give her another chance, and this had seemed like the only way.

Otherwise, what would she do? Go home to Connecticut? Then what? Go back to the studio where she had first learned to dance? Get a job teaching the little girls? Or just keep practicing, go out on auditions this winter and spring? But how would she explain her sudden and unceremonious departure to prospective employers? Should she leave her brief stint as a trainee off her resume? She knew how small the ballet world was. Her reputation as a flake, as *unreliable*, would precede her everywhere she went.

But what did she want, if not ballet? She was nineteen, turning twenty soon. She'd never taken the SATs, the ACTs. She'd done the bare minimum to graduate from her online high school. Would she have to live at home, go to community college? And study what?

What had she wanted to be before ballet?

She could barely remember anymore what it felt like to have a wide-open future ahead of her. Second grade, maybe? She had a vague recollection of an "All About Me" project she did at the beginning of the school year: *My name is Alexia Adams. I am eight years old. My favorite food is pizza. My favorite color is lilac. When I grow up I want to be an artist.*

Had she really wanted to be an artist? She remembered liking to paint and draw. Her father was an artist, after all; she'd grown up surrounded by art. He took her into the city to go to museums: The Guggenheim, MoMA, the Met.

What she did remember was her mother's reaction to the poster that hung on the wall of her classroom on open house day. Alex had been proud of the self-portrait she'd made. Of how hard she'd worked to make individual strands of hair rather than just a black blob.

Her mother had read the list excitedly, stopping at the last statement. She hadn't said anything at all, about how realistic the eyes' pupils looked or about the way Alex had exactly recreated her favorite T-shirt, the one with the daisies on it.

In the car on the way home that afternoon, her mother had been quiet.

"I thought you wanted to be a *dancer*," she'd said.

"Daddy says I'm good at art," she says. "Right, Daddy?"

"Our next Georgia O'Keeffe!" he said, and smiled at her.

Her mother stiffened and was quiet for a long time. Alex had looked out the window at the colorful leaves, like a fiery collage. She thought about how she might paint them; what colors she would use.

"Drew . . ." her mother started. But then stopped. She stared straight ahead at the road, not even noticing how beautiful the trees were.

When she turned to look at Alex in the back seat, her face had softened.

"Dancing is an art, too, you know. Dancers are artists."

After that, Alex had continued drawing and sketching in

books she kept in her desk drawer. After her father moved out, they would paint side by side in his studio. She never shared this with her mother. What was the point?

Now, she tried to imagine going home. Living in her childhood bedroom with its pink curtains and poster of Misty Copeland hanging on the wall. Her first pair of ballet shoes preserved behind glass. Her mother shuffling around, asking questions, demanding answers. Her disappointment as thick as fog. Her failure would live in the house with them, an unwelcome houseguest who wouldn't leave.

"Alexia?" Nicholai said, and she returned from whatever faraway place she had gone. It was the same place she had been right before she walked off the stage, she thought.

"Yes," she said. "I'm sorry."

"You are injured?"

"Yes, yes. Nothing serious, a sprain, I think? I twisted it right at the beginning of Snow. I didn't know what to do," she said. At least this was true. Her mind had not known what to do, while her body had been determined to flee.

He scowled, and she kept rambling.

"I think I was in shock? I didn't even realize what happened until I got backstage; then it started to swell, and by the time I got home, it was bruised. I am going home the day after Christmas. I'll go to my doctor. Get an X-ray."

She thought of her family doctor, the rheumy-eyed Dr. Nickerson, who should have retired ages ago. She saw him only for the annual checkups required for her summer intensives. She was a terrible liar.

"No," he said, pushing his chair back from the desk and standing up. "If you are injured, you must see Maria today."

Her eyes widened. Was he giving her her job back? Had this worked? He certainly wouldn't send her to PT if she was no longer a trainee.

"Does this mean I can stay?" she asked.

But then she thought about going into Maria's office, jumping up onto the crinkly paper on the table. About presenting her with a perfectly good foot. Maria would know Alex had been lying. And she would go back to Nicholai.

"I really do think it's okay," she continued before he could answer. "I just put the boot on to stabilize it. I promise, I'll see my doctor at home. I should be fine by the time break is over."

Nicholai loomed over his desk, meaty palms pressed against the wood. When did he get so big?

"Alexia. You know that you are gifted, yes?"

She didn't know what the correct answer was. Should she confidently acknowledge his praise or humbly refuse it? The first might make her seem arrogant; the latter might make her seem like a child.

"Ulyana, she worries about you."

This made her feel awful. Ulyana, everyone's favorite teacher, a second mother to them all.

"She says you are only going through the motions. That your body complies, but that your mind is elsewhere."

She didn't know how to respond to this, either.

"A gift is not to be squandered," he said.

She nodded. If she agreed, if she promised, maybe he would let her come back?

"See Maria," he said. Not a recommendation, but a stipulation. An ultimatum.

An *order*.

Sofia

In the quiet parlor, the old woman sat across the table from Sofia and studied her face. Around the woman's neck, the Christmas-light necklace beat an unsteady rhythm, the red and green lights mesmerizing. When the psychic reached across the table, beckoning for Sofia's hand, Sofia reluctantly complied.

The woman's hands were remarkably warm and soft. And she held Sofia's gently in her own as if cradling a small bird.

"*You* are lost," the woman said.

"*No*," she said, wondering if this woman might be suffering from dementia herself. Sofia had already clarified she was looking for someone else. "Like I said before, someone *close* to me is lost. And I need to find her. So anything you can tell me that would send me in the right direction would be appreciated. Also, I'm not sure how long this takes, but I actually don't have a whole lot of time. Sorry." Sofia felt foolish; why was she wasting time here?

The woman peered at Sofia over her bright red cheaters. Her eyes were milky with cataracts, and Sofia tried to imagine how she might appear to her through those filmy lenses.

"Okay," the woman said. "Quick read, missing mom, got it."

"I didn't say mom."

"You didn't?" she said.

"Nope."

"But she's the one you're looking for, right?"

What point was there in being coy now? In the interest of time, she said, "Yes."

The woman closed her eyes, and for a moment, Sofia worried she had fallen asleep, her lips slightly parted, her breathing heavy.

"Listen," Sofia offered. "If it helps at all, I know she has a suitcase with her."

The woman opened her eyes. "It's not a suitcase."

"Yes, it is. Giuseppe at the Italian market saw her this morning, and she had a suitcase. She told him she was meeting someone."

"This happened a long time ago," the woman said.

"No," Sofia said. "It happened this morning."

The woman shook her head, insistent. "No, no, no. All of this was before."

"Before *what*?" Sofia asked, losing her patience.

"Before *you*."

Sofia shook her hand loose from the woman's grip and took a deep breath, the same breathing she encouraged her clients to do both during and after giving birth. A cleansing breath. But it did little to squash the fluttery sensation in her chest.

Who was this quack? And why was she wasting her time here? *Precious* time that she could be out searching.

"This is not helpful," she said, starting to rise from the hard-backed chair where she was sitting.

"I hear a train," the woman said, closing her eyes.

Oh, lord.

"Like a subway train?"

"I'm not sure," the woman said, and Sofia waited. Worried, she wondered if her mother had somehow managed to procure a MetroCard without her wallet. Jumped a turnstile? Perhaps someone had let her borrow their own card or bought one for her. New Yorkers could be prickly folks, but they also kept an eye out for one another. She had been banking on that since the alert went out.

"Any idea which line? Do you see a color or a number or letter or anything? Is it, like, going to Brooklyn or uptown?"

"Wait, I do see a number," the woman said. *Of course, she did.* "Two numbers. Eighty-nine and forty-two. Is your mother eighty-nine?"

"She's eighty," Sofia said, exasperated.

"Are you forty-two?"

Sofia could barely remember forty-two. More than a decade ago now. She should be flattered, but then again, the woman's vision could not be great.

"Nope."

"I'm sorry," the woman said, and sat back in her overstuffed armchair with a sigh, rubbing her temples.

Sofia waited, then figured maybe it would be best if she just gave her all the info that she had. Really, she had no reason (or time) to play games. She was here for this self-proclaimed *seer* to help *her* see more clearly.

Sofia thought about the note, that creamy stationery, and her mother's careful note to her father. "Listen, she left a note for my father—who's dead, by the way—that she was going out to get something special for Christmas."

"Yes. She has a gift," the woman said.

"Do you know where she went to buy it?"

The woman shook her head. "No. It is inside that case."

Sofia's shoulders slumped. Did her mother have a suitcase or not? And if so, why would she be carrying the gift inside it? None of this made any sense.

"Listen, I really need to go," she said. "Thank you for your time. How much do I owe you?"

"Twenty bucks," the woman said matter-of-factly.

Sofia pulled a twenty-dollar bill from her wallet and placed it on the table, wondering what the rules for tipping were when it came to psychics, and pulled out another five. She tightened her scarf around her neck and turned to go. The room had grown darker, the sky outside the window heavy with clouds. The room glowed softly in the Tiffany lamp's twilight. For a moment, Sofia felt disoriented. As if she'd stumbled into the parlor of a turn-of-the-century brothel.

"Wait," the woman said, her eyes bright with understanding. "I see a clock."

"A watch? Is the gift a watch?"

"Look for the clock. You will find her there."

This woman really was just pulling things out of thin air now, hoping something would stick. Trains and gifts and suitcases and clocks. What a sham.

Though, to be fair, the clairvoyant had gotten a few things right. That her mother was missing. That she had procured some sort of gift. And maybe, even, that her mother was not only lost in the city, but lost in time, as well.

Sofia remembered the alert. Of course. The "psychic" had probably gotten the alert on her phone along with the rest of the city. Saw a missing woman with dementia and hedged her bets that Sofia might be her daughter.

But how did that explain her mother's perfume, the scent not much more than a memory now as she opened the door?

"Before *you*," the woman had said.

Was it possible her mother not only thought that her father was still alive, but that Sofia not yet was? And if that were true, where had she gone?

Alex

Alex stood in front of the fountain in the courtyard at Lincoln Center and had no idea where she should go. She couldn't go see Maria in PT. Maria would know the second she removed the boot that there was nothing wrong with her ankle. No swelling. No bruising. No sprain or broken bone. She hadn't even twisted it. She would send her back to Nicholai, who would know she had lied to him. Could you lose your job twice?

This had been a horrible idea.

Nicholai had made her feel selfish. Walking off stage. Watching other dancers struggle when it came easily to her. Why couldn't she love it the way they did? Some of her friends, like Zu-Zu, lived and breathed ballet. From the moment she woke up in the morning, Zu-Zu was abuzz with excitement for what the day held. Zu-Zu *loved* class, the endless hours at the barre, and the grueling rehearsals that sometimes went into the night. And performances were the sweet buttercream frosting on the ballet cake for these girls. But Alex could never understand it. The work at the barre felt boring; the same combinations again and again and again. Her body memorized them, and she was on autopilot most days, not fully waking up until the *grand battements*. Because trainees only got corps roles (and even then, only if they were very lucky), rehearsals were an exercise in patience. Some days, she'd spend the entire rehearsal just marking on the side. Performances, of course, were exciting. But going onstage also made her feel slightly uneasy; so much pressure. Though she couldn't see her, she knew her mother was out there, wringing her hands, holding her breath. It was paralyzing. That is exactly what it had felt like last night.

But she had no words to explain this to her mother. No way to tell her that sometimes her life felt suffocating. She had read once about the archaic practice of Chinese foot binding. Seen photos of how these poor women's feet grew deformed, stunted inside their wrappings. Butterflies stuck inside their cocoons. How could she tell her mother that she felt trapped in this gilded cage?

And so, year after year, she moved forward, encouraged by teachers, plucked out of auditions by directors, cast by these same directors in parts other dancers would die for. What was wrong with her?

Nicholai's words resounded in her head, like marbles in a metal bowl. *A gift is not to be squandered.*

She flashed on a memory of a birthday party when she was in elementary school. She didn't know the little girl very well, but those were the days when birthday parties involved entire classrooms. It had been held at a local pizza place, and for hours, she and her classmates had played the arcade games, the tickets spit out of the noisy machines exchanged for tchotchkes and stuffed animals. She had won the jackpot on a race-car game and turned in her tickets for a bright purple dinosaur toy, which she set down by her plate when they all gathered at the long table for pizza and cake. When the food was gone, an employee wheeled over the cart, where they had put their wrapped presents. She had worried about the gift from the moment they bought it. She had wanted to get the girl a Lego set or Matchbox cars, but her mother had insisted on the Barbie doll. When the birthday girl got to her gift, she felt her throat tighten, and as she had feared, the girl opened the sparkly doll and scowled, mumbled a *thank you* at her mother's insistence, then tossed the doll down and moved on to the next gift.

Alex felt a hand on her shoulder and turned to see her mother fuming.

"I have never seen a more ungrateful child," her mother said, loud enough for the other mothers to hear.

"Maybe she doesn't like dolls," Alex whispered, mortified. She knew for a fact that the girl did not like dolls. She had tried to tell her mother this as they stood in the Barbie aisle at Target.

"Every girl likes Barbies," her mother had argued.

Alex had started to say that *she* didn't like dolls, either, but she had also felt that, while her mom's words were sharp, she seemed more hurt than mad.

Her mother had waited for her by the door to say goodbye to her friends and to the birthday girl. Alex felt the dinosaur's soft fur in her hand and knew she had no choice but to offer it to her classmate. And as much as she had wanted to keep it, as she said goodbye, she glanced toward her mother, who was busy with her phone, and handed it to her.

The girl looked surprised.

"I'm sorry that Barbie wasn't what you wanted. I tried to tell my mom."

This wasn't what she wanted. It was as simple as that. For the last sixteen years, she had been doing something she didn't, really, want to do. And for what? For whom?

Her mom. How was she going to tell her mother? She tried to imagine her response, and her stomach twisted.

As if Alex had summoned her, a text chimed on her phone.

Thinking about you. How is your foot?

She sat down at the fountain's stony edge, feeling its frigid spray, then realized that the cold water was coming from the sky. The confectioners'-sugar snow from earlier had turned to an icy rain.

The courtyard at Lincoln Center was empty. In a couple of hours, it would fill with patrons coming to see *The Nutcracker* matinee. There would be mothers and their daughters, dressed in their Christmas dresses. Emerald and ruby taffeta. Sparkly shoes. There would be fur-collared coats and fuzzy muffs to keep small hands warm. There would be the little girls, hoping to meet the Sugar Plum Fairy at the stage door after the performance.

She remembered the first time she had come to the city to see *The Nutcracker*. They were supposed to go as a family, but her parents had been arguing. She didn't know what it was about at the time, but later she would understand that it had been just one of many arguments that led to her father's departure. And so that night, she and her mother had driven into the city alone. Her mother hated driving in Manhattan, and had been a nervous wreck the whole way, gripping the steering wheel as if she were holding on for dear life. And during the performance, she had clutched Alex's hand with the same ferocity. After the show, her tiny bones had ached from her mother's excitement.

She looked at the text from her mom and took a deep breath.

Not dancing the rest of the shows. Nicholai wants me to see Maria.

The truth, but somehow, it still felt like a lie.

Sofia

When she opened the clairvoyant's door to the street, she was met with a strong gust of wind, and the earlier flurries of snow had turned to freezing rain. She hadn't brought an umbrella.

"Take one," the woman said, finally reading her mind, motioning to an umbrella stand by the door where at least half a dozen forgotten umbrellas stood expectantly.

"Thank you," she said, plucking a bright red one from the bunch. At least she'd gotten something for her twenty-five dollars.

She thought again about walking to Washington Square Park. But as lost as her mother might be in her own mind, she couldn't imagine that she would willingly sit outside in this weather.

No, wherever she was, she was likely inside. Still, she had no idea where to go next. Her mother's note had said she had gone to get something special for Christmas, and the seer had concurred that there was some kind of gift. And that the gift was in that suitcase.

Sofia tried to remember the other gifts her mother had given her father for Christmas over the years. The Irish wool sweater from Dublin when she was performing in the British Isles. The bottle of Glengoyne single malt Scotch sent from a distillery in the highlands of Scotland. The beautiful soft leather bag from the streets of Rome. The wooden backgammon set from Mykonos. Sofia and her father had sat together by the fire that Christmas, playing backgammon and listening to the recording of her mother's symphony from the prior Christmas when she had been in Prague.

But when she was in New York, where did her mother shop for gifts? Sofia tried to think. Thoughts of Christmas conjured Macy's, of course; every year, her father had taken her to Santa-land to see the lights and meet Santa. This was where he would shop for gifts for her mother, as well. That Jean Patou perfume. The chocolate-colored cashmere scarf she wore until the moths riddled it with holes. The silky robe and the delicate pair of emerald earrings. But her mother didn't like department stores; they were overwhelming to her. She preferred the boutiques found in Greenwich Village.

Perhaps Sofia should go home, duck into all the shops along the way, ask if the proprietors had seen her. By now, most of them would have received the alert and would be keeping an eye out. But if that were the case, certainly someone would have notified the police, right?

Her own phone had rung with alerts several times before: photos of elderly people who had wandered away. She'd felt palpable relief when the follow-up alerts announced that the wanderers had been found safely. She hadn't dared to ask the woman at the precinct what the success rate was. Did they all come home eventually? But what about those who didn't? Where did they go?

At home, she would wait for her mother to wander back. She'd read a story once about a dog that traveled over 2500 miles home to its family in Oregon after being lost while the family was visiting relatives in Indiana. Certainly, her mother would be able to make her way back to the apartment where she had lived for the last fifty years.

Her phone buzzed again, and hope rose in her throat that her mother, like Bobbie the Wonder Dog, had somehow navigated her way through the labyrinth of her muddy mind home. She pulled her phone from her bag and saw her mother's caretaker Constance's name on the screen.

"Constance," she said, accepting the call, feeling the instant sense of calm Constance always evoked. Sofia wondered if she gave her own clients the same sense of peace.

"Oh my God, Sofia," Constance said, her voice cracking. "I just saw the alert on my phone. I'm coming over."

"It's Christmas Eve, Constance," she said, though she felt gratitude, warm and liquid, in her chest.

"You think I need to watch *A Christmas Story* for the hundredth time?" she said. "Besides, the boys got their big gift early—it's a PlayStation—it'll keep them busy all day. I don't need to be home until mass tonight."

"Okay. I'll meet you at the apartment."

"Give me twenty minutes," Constance said. "Don't worry. We'll find your sweet mama."

"Hey," Sofia said before she hung up. "Did Mom say anything to you about going on a trip? Giuseppe said she had a suitcase with her."

"No," she said. "But didn't she travel a lot? Before? She probably just got confused."

"Yes," Sofia said. "I guess you're right. Especially around the holidays."

She was always gone.

On the way back to the apartment, she stopped into a cheese shop, a rare book shop, three clothing boutiques, and a toy shop. None of the clerks had seen her mother, and only two had received the alert.

"There's a silver alert," she said, exasperated, to the young woman, who was working behind the counter at the toy shop, which was packed with frazzled parents searching for last-minute stocking stuffers for their children. "See," she had implored, showing her the alert on her phone, the photo of her mother that had to be at least fifteen years old: her professional headshot, taken before she retired.

"I'm sorry, ma'am," the clerk said impatiently, as a woman pushed past Sofia and loaded the counter with toys. "I really need to help our customers."

Sofia slipped away from the counter, spying a small stuffed rabbit on a display. She grabbed it and returned to the counter. She would bring this with her once she was able to get to her clients' house to check in on Dana and baby.

As the woman rang her up, she tried one last pitch. "Her name is Simone De Luca. The violinist?" As if her mother's credentials might somehow elicit sympathy.

The woman put the bunny in tissue, then in a striped sack.

"I hope you find her," she said, softening for a moment. "Happy holidays."

Back at the apartment building, Sofia saw that the brick holding open the door had been removed. That meant Constance was likely already here. Or, perhaps, her mother had made her way home? Or maybe some desperate thief had found his way in.

She fumbled for her keys, opened then closed the door behind her, and shook the wet umbrella before leaving it in the foyer. She took the steep steps two at a time up to the apartment, where the door was closed and locked.

"Mom?" she asked.

But when the door opened, it was Constance, with her warm smile and embrace.

"Oh, honey," Constance said, pulling back and studying Simone's face.

"She's not here?" Sofia asked, gazing over Constance's shoulder into the living room.

"No," Constance said. "But I found something."

Sofia tried to imagine what sort of clue her mother had left behind. Perhaps Constance had found the note.

Inside the house, which was stifling, Sofia removed her coat and slipped off her wet shoes.

"What did you find?"

"It's actually what's *missing*," Constance said.

Sofia cocked her head. What did she mean?

"She took her violin."

"Her violin?"

"It's usually right next to your father's desk in the attic. But it's not there. I've looked everywhere."

The *suitcase* Giuseppe had mentioned. The psychic had said it wasn't a suitcase she was carrying, but that there was a "gift" inside the case. Had the woman been right? Was Simone carrying her violin case? If so, where would she be going with her violin?

"This happened a long time ago," the clairvoyant had offered. "Before you."

A gift, a clock. 89, 42. Maybe she shouldn't have been so dismissive of her clues.

She ran upstairs to the third floor and found the note where she'd left it.

Darling, I've gone to pick up something special for Christmas. Don't follow me. It's a surprise. Yours until the stars fall from the sky, Simone.

Where was she?

"Someone's calling your phone!" Constance hollered from downstairs.

Sofia raced down the stairs, practically tumbling on the last three steps.

Her phone vibrated on the kitchen table. An unfamiliar number. *Please let it be the police.*

"Hello?" she said.

"Hi, Sofia, this is Christopher. I thought you'd want to know that we took the baby to the hospital. Everything's okay. But they think she might have RSV. They're doing some tests."

"Okay," she said, conjuring every bit of calm and serenity she could muster. "Please let Dana know it's going to be okay. RSV is very common, and in newborns, the risk of severe infection is low. You were smart to go to the ER. They will take good care of her."

"I know it's Christmas Eve, and Dana said you have something going on with your family, but I know it would help her a lot to see you. I feel like I'm just making things worse."

"Okay," she said. "Where are you?"

"Lenox Health," he said. "On Seventh."

Lenox Health was where St. Vincent's used to be, only a half mile from here. She could be there in ten minutes. Then it hit her, like a fist to the chest. The hospital. She hadn't called the hospitals. Was it possible someone had found her mother and brought her to a hospital?

She pulled her boots and coat back on and said, "I'm going to St. Vincent's."

"Oh no. Is it your mom?" Constance said, her hand pressed against her chest.

"No, no. At least I don't think so. It's one of my clients. But maybe Mom wound up there, too?"

"Okay. I'll stay here. Call me if you hear anything?"

"Of course."

Outside, the temperature had dropped further, and the sidewalks were already starting to grow icy. If her mother hadn't slipped and fallen yet, she was certain to. Despite the slick ground, Sofia walked briskly, then started to jog along Charles Street to Seventh Avenue to the hospital.

Alex

Alex had told Zu-Zu she would meet her back at Lincoln Center after the matinee. It was two-thirty now; she had at least an hour and a half to kill before the show was over.

She wondered if she actually *could* go to Maria's office, tell her what had happened. Just explain she'd made a terrible mistake. That she'd lost herself onstage. But Maria was no therapist. The dancers jokingly called her "The Punisher," her office filled with torture devices. Maria was only five feet tall, but she was intimidating. Relentless. She was also not one for chit-chat. Her solitary goal was making a dancer's body well, to ensure that they could continue enduring the rigors of rehearsals and performance. Why couldn't they have someone there to help when a dancer's mind felt strained, sprained, bruised, or broken? Someone who could pay as much attention to their hearts as their hamstrings? She couldn't go see Maria.

She looked down at her boot and felt foolish. She wanted to take it off and hurl it into the fountain. But she hadn't brought a second shoe, so she was stuck with it, at least until she got back to the apartment. But thinking about her apartment made her chest ache. She thought of her drawers filled with leotards and tights. Her windowsill with her pointe shoes lined up like pink satin soldiers. The portable barre behind the door, the Harvey Edwards poster of a pair of feet in fifth position, tattered leg warmers and duct-taped ballet shoes. It was only a poster, of course, not a print, but her mother had somehow managed to get it signed by the photographer. It had hung over her bed for years, and her mother insisted she bring it to New York when she and Zu-Zu got their apartment. A reminder that ballet was work first. A reminder that it was supposed to be a grind.

Her stomach rumbled, and she realized she hadn't eaten since this morning. Once, she'd forgotten to eat breakfast before class and almost passed out during *adagio*. She needed to be clear-headed, not light-headed, right now.

As she walked down the broad steps from the plaza to Columbus, she realized this could actually be it. Her last time at Lincoln Center. Her last day in the city. She'd been here for years now, and suddenly, it was *over*.

If she left, there would be no more acai bowls with Zu-Zu and their friend, Bea, at their favorite smoothie place. No more movies at the pier on hot summer nights. No more picnics in Central Park and no more window-shopping on Fifth Avenue. Her life, as she knew it, was *ending*.

When she had toyed with the idea of quitting before, it had felt dangerous but exciting. But now that the prospect was becoming a reality, the idea of losing everything else made her feel hollowed out. What had made the hard work and long days worth it had been this: the city, her friends. But without ballet, the city no longer belonged to her.

She was overwhelmed with nostalgia. Nostalgia for her own life. She wanted to collect the city up into her pocket and carry it with her. Everything she loved about it here. For the last couple of years, it had been her home.

Hobbling up Columbus, she saw the *creperie* where she and Zu-Zu would go after long days in rehearsals. Zu-Zu loved the savory crepes with mushrooms and peppers and vegan cheese. Alex preferred the Nutella and strawberry ones; she ordered one now from the guy behind the counter, the boy Zu-Zu thought was cute.

"Where's your friend?" he asked, pouring the batter onto the hot griddle.

She and Zu-Zu were always together; she never did this alone.

"She's performing," she said.

He expertly flipped the crepe as though he were making an origami animal, and slipped it into a paper cone when she said she wanted it *to go*.

"Here you are; extra Nutella," he said, and handed it to her.

When she reached for her wallet, he looked behind him to make sure no one was paying attention, and said, "It's on the house. Merry Christmas."

Outside, the rain was coming down in icy shards, but somehow, it made her feel alive. Grounded. She worried that if not for this, she might float up into that cloudy sky.

She made her way to the bus stop on Broadway, eating the crepe quickly, feeling the warmth of it spread through her. On the nearly empty M5 bus, she sat down across from an old woman whose face looked familiar for some reason, and they smiled at each other. She took this bus home from NYRB nearly every day; she'd probably seen her before.

The woman was wearing a beautiful black coat with furry trim, the lapels embroidered with red roses and curling green vines. Her silvery hair was in two braids pinned up. Her face was elegant and her eyes kind. At her feet was a case, for an instrument, maybe?

When she was in school, Alex had wanted to play the cello. She'd pleaded with her mother to let her take lessons. There was something so beautiful about both the instrument and the music it made.

"When would you have time for that?" her mother had asked.

This was in seventh grade, and she was dancing six days a week by then. Whenever she brought up things she might like to do—go horseback riding, have a birthday party, go to a school dance, go to sleepovers—her mother had responded in the same way. "When?" or "How?" There were only so many hours in the day, and the ones that did not belong to school belonged to ballet. She thought of her life like one of those pie charts. A slice for school, a slice for sleep, and the rest of the pie all ballet. What was left in the pie plate when you took ballet away?

She thought about asking the woman where she was going, but striking up a conversation with a total stranger on a bus was something you weren't supposed to do. Though it *was* Christmas Eve, and the woman was all alone.

"Are you a musician?" Alex asked tentatively, gesturing to the case with her chin.

The woman's eyes widened, and she nodded.

"Oh! Where do you play?" she asked. "I'm a dancer, at NYRB," she said, then felt a sinking sensation in her chest. "I mean, I used to be."

The woman looked at her boot with sympathy, probably assuming she'd been taken out by an injury.

"I don't know what I would do if I couldn't play," the woman said. "It would be as if someone told me I wasn't allowed to breathe."

Her words felt like strings plucking in Alex's chest. Ballet had never felt like this for her. Elemental as air. She'd never felt that way about anything at all.

"I'd *love* to play for the ballet's orchestra one day," the woman said, her eyes alight, hand pressed to her chest.

What a strange dream for an old woman to have. Was it even possible to begin a career at her age? She didn't know about musicians, but dancers needed to train from the time they were little. After a certain point, it simply wasn't a possibility anymore.

This thought made her feel panic creeping in. Was it too late for her to start over? She was only nineteen, but she felt like an old woman whose life had passed her by.

"I just moved here in June," the woman said, her cheeks pink and eyes bright.

"Oh!" Alex said. "Well, welcome to New York!"

As they drove along the bottom of the park, the air between them grew quiet.

"I've been busking at Rockefeller Plaza," the woman said. "But it's too cold for that today. My fingers don't work when it's this cold."

And Alex thought about Rockefeller Plaza, about the towering tree and the skaters and the lights. She hadn't had any time to go see it with rehearsals and performances nearly every night. She could go there one last time. It was Christmas Eve, after all.

When the bus arrived at Fifth Avenue and West 50th Street, Alex stood, reaching for a strap to keep herself steady, no small feat on one foot.

"I hope you have a nice Christmas," the woman said. "Maybe someday we'll perform together at the Met."

And for some reason, Alex felt like crying.

"Do you have someone to spend Christmas with?" Alex asked, thinking of this elderly woman alone on Christmas Eve.

"Yes!" she said. "My husband. We're newlyweds. This is our first Christmas together."

"Oh," Alex said, surprised. A newlywed, too. How funny, to start your life over as an old woman. How brave.

"I have a special gift for him," the old woman said. "But I have to meet someone first."

Alex tilted her head, waiting for more. But the bus doors opened. If she didn't get out, she'd miss the stop.

"Merry Christmas," Alex said, hobbling down the steps and onto Fifth Avenue.

Sofia

Sofia had never liked hospitals, and this aversion became worse after her father's illness. Fortunately, most of her clients gave birth at home, and she hadn't set foot in a hospital in several months. But here she was now at Lenox Health.

She went to the woman at the information desk and asked if there was any way she could check to see if an elderly patient had been admitted. She explained about the silver alert and showed her the photo of her mother. The woman was polite and made a few calls on the blinking phone, but in the end, shrugged. "We don't seem to have had any new admittances that match her description."

It had been a long shot, she knew. And she suspected that the hospitals had also received the alerts.

"Is there anything else I can help you with?" the woman asked.

"I'm actually here to check in on one of my clients. I'm a doula, and my client came in with her newborn just a bit ago."

"They're probably in the ER," the woman said, her face filled with pity. A missing mother and an ill infant; Sofia really was a disaster.

She followed the woman's directions to the ER, through the labyrinthine hallways, which bore that distinct scent of disinfectant and hospital cafeteria food. It was the smell of her father's last days. Her stomach turned. If she'd had anything in it, she might have wanted to vomit.

In the ER, she saw several people waiting to be seen, and soon spotted Christopher, sitting at the edge of his seat, with his hands clasped between his knees, staring up at a TV showing *It's a Wonderful Life.*

She sat down next to him and touched his shoulder. He startled, but as soon as he realized that she wasn't a doctor come to deliver bad news, he seemed to relax.

"How is she?" she asked.

"The baby? Or Dana?"

"Both," she said.

"They're still running tests. They ruled out RSV, at least," he said.

"Oh, that's wonderful," she said, feeling a surge of relief. "How are *you*?"

"Terrified," he said, and his face flushed red, as if he were ashamed to admit his weakness.

She squeezed his hand. And in that moment, she recalled the time she broke her arm when she was a kid. Her mother had been out of town, and her father had run an errand, leaving her in the apartment alone. He'd locked her in and made her promise not to answer the door for anyone. He'd taught her how to lock the security chain, putting a stepstool by the door so she could reach.

When he was gone, she had tiptoed to her parents' room and studied the big bed, the one she was forbidden from jumping on. But her mother wasn't here; she was in Vienna. And her father was at least two blocks away, grabbing the Sunday paper. And so, she'd climbed up.

But only two or three good bounces in, her foot had slipped

off the edge of the bed, and she'd landed, palm first on the floor, pain shooting up her arm. She had lain on the floor, terrified not only by the pain, but by what would happen when her dad came home and knocked their secret knock, and she wouldn't be able to unlock the door.

Somehow, she'd managed to drag herself to the living room when he finally came home a few moments later, and he'd scooped her up in his arms and carried her down the stairs and all the way to the ER, as though it was her leg that she had broken instead of her arm.

For hours, they had sat at the hospital, waiting to be seen. And her father kept disappearing outside to use the pay phone to try to reach her mother. But it was six hours later in Vienna, and her mother was performing. He couldn't get in touch with her until late that afternoon, when they were back at home with Sofia cozy on the couch, wearing a brand-new cast, and a bowl of her father's famous homemade minestrone before her on a TV tray.

She had heard her father's hushed conversation with her mother in the other room.

"No, no. She's fine. You don't need to come home," he said.

Silence.

"Oh, honey, don't cry."

The idea of her mother crying had felt so foreign to her. Her mother was stoic and serious. She never cried. She hadn't even cried at Sofia's grandmother's funeral.

"Simone," he said. "It's not your fault. You're a good mother."

Christopher had returned to staring blankly at the TV screen, with Jimmy Stewart running down the snowy street hollering "Merry Christmas" to all of Bedford Falls, having realized that he had, indeed, made a difference in the lives of his family, of his community.

"Do you think they'll let me see her?" Sofia asked.

"Oh," he said, turning to her as if he'd forgotten she was there. "Let me text her," he said, and pulled his phone out. "Shoot. There's no service in here. Hold on."

He got up and went to the nurse's station, and when he came back, he said that they would let Dana know that she was here.

There was no cell service here. What if the police tried to reach out? Her mother wasn't at this hospital, but she might be at another one.

When Dana entered the waiting room, she came straight to Sofia, who stood up, opened her arms, and pulled her in. Dana's body trembled and shuddered, and she pulled away, wiping furiously at her tears. Sofia thought she had makeup smudged under her eyes, but soon realized it was just dark circles. The poor new mom probably hadn't seen any sleep since the baby was born. She should be at home, resting.

"Tell me what the doctors are saying," Sofia said, trying to bring Dana back to herself.

Dana explained that they were running more tests. That it wasn't RSV. That she seemed to be breathing okay and was running only a mild fever.

"How can I be screwing it up already?" she said, her eyes seeking something from Sofia.

"Oh, honey, no," she said. "You haven't done anything wrong. You did everything right. Bringing her here was the smart thing to do. She's in good hands, and I bet you'll be home before the sun goes down tonight. How are *you* feeling?"

Dana nodded. "I'm okay."

"Is there anything I can do for you? In the meantime?" she asked.

Dana breathed in and blubbered out a shuddering sob. "I'm really *hungry*," she said.

"Well, I can certainly get food. What would you like?"

"A cheeseburger?" she said. "But only if you have time. You had a family emergency?"

"It's okay. I have time. Let me get you both some food."

"The cafeteria food is terrible," Dana said. "But I think there's a burger place down the street. Is that awful? Should I not be eating fast food?"

"You should be eating whatever you are craving," Sofia said. "What kind of burger do you want?"

"Double cheeseburger, extra pickles? Are you sure that's not awful?"

"It sounds delicious," she said. "Go back to your baby. We'll come get you once I have the food," she said. She took Christopher's order and headed outside.

As soon as she exited the building and had cell reception, her phone began to buzz with alert after alert. Missed call. Missed call. Text messages. She saw the burger joint less than a block away and rushed through the sleet to the entrance.

Inside the warm restaurant, her stomach rumbled at the smell of French fries and burgers. She gave the order for Dana and Christopher and ordered a cheeseburger for herself. She sat down and quickly devoured the burger, checking her phone for everything she'd missed.

Heart quaking, she pressed on the first missed call.

It was another client, due any day now, giving her an update ("a few Braxton Hicks, but nothing yet!") and holiday greetings. The text was from her mother's primary doctor, reminding her of an appointment next week.

The second call was from a New York number she didn't recognize.

"Hi, Ms. De Luca, this is Deputy Commissioner O'Hara from the Sixth Precinct. I wanted to let you know we've had a few sightings that our officers are following up on. We just got a tip from someone who said she they saw an elderly woman matching her description getting off the bus near Forty-Second Street."

What on earth would she be doing on 42nd Street?

Wait. *42*, the psychic had said. Was it possible? Could she have meant 42nd Street? What was the other number? *89*. That was it.

Trying to remember to chew, she quickly typed in *89, 42nd Street* into her map app, selected the address, and zoomed in.

Grand Central Terminal.

Alex

At Rockefeller Plaza, Alex stood watching the three ice skaters willing to brave the freezing rain as they circled the rink, the golden statue of Prometheus glowing in the light of the towering tree. In all the time she'd lived in New York, she'd never gone skating here. She'd never gone skating anywhere, as a matter of fact. Back at home, there was a rink where kids often had their birthday parties, but she had never been allowed to attend. Skating was risky; a broken ankle or wrist could take her out of ballet for weeks.

Once, when her best friend turned eleven, she had pleaded to go, promised her mother she would just watch. "*Nutcracker* is in a month," her mother had said. She was cast as Clara in her studio's production that year. An injury of any kind would mean that she wouldn't be able to perform.

At least she'd be able to have cake and see her friends outside of school. But sitting alone on the bench, watching her friends and classmates through the glass, she had never felt as lonely. They skated and fell, laughed and chased each other. None of the other kids were thinking beyond the moment. A broken wrist would mean a cast for friends to sign, and getting out of PE for six weeks. She remembered sitting on the carpeted bench seat, feeling her chest tighten.

She had been watching the entire world behind glass. All these years.

Her eyes stung as she considered all she had missed. All the lives she hadn't lived. The idea of starting over.

Then she thought about everything her mother had sacrificed over the years, and she started to feel sick. Her mother's martyrdom was never spoken of, but it hung between them like a ghost. When Alex was little, her mother spent every bit of free time she had driving Alex to ballet class and competitions, to master classes in the city. She stayed up late sewing tutus, a skill she learned to save them money when it came time for her to start doing variations. After Alex was accepted into NYRB's school, she had started her consulting business so she could afford the tuition.

But Alex had never asked for it. Never asked for any of it.

The Christmas tree at the top of the rink reminded her of the tree in *The Nutcracker*, the one that grew and grew. When she'd gone to see the ballet in the city, it had felt magical. She had fallen into Drosselmeyer's spell. But when she began to perform on that same stage, she quickly learned that it was all an illusion. Pulleys and hydraulics controlled the tree. The snow that fell from the "sky" onto the swirling snowflakes below was swept up after each performance. It was a dream for everyone but those on and behind the stage.

What did *she* want?

For her whole life so far, she'd been told it was this. *Believed* it was this.

The lights on the tree blurred, and she realized she was weeping.

Sofia

Grand Central Terminal? Was Simone planning to get on a train? Sofia quickly delivered the food to Christopher and promised to check back in on Dana and the baby as soon as possible. But as she made her way to the subway station, she kicked herself for having wasted so much time between Giuseppe and the psychic, then the hospital. Though Giuseppe had set her on this path to begin with, and the psychic may have given her the key to solve this mystery. And visiting Dana and Christopher at the hospital was her job. A job that she took seriously. Certainly, her mother would understand that.

She thought about the other sacrifices she had made for her work. She had never had her own children, for one. Of course, this was, in part, because she'd never found anyone she wanted to have children with. Not that that would have stopped her, of course. But as a single mother, she couldn't imagine how she would have managed to be a parent with her unpredictable schedule; she couldn't exactly leave a child home alone in the middle of the night while she tended to her clients. But really, she hadn't had children, made a family, because of her mother.

198 / Tammy Greenwood

Sofia hadn't wanted her child to grow up as she had: her mother a shadow, a wish, a *myth*. At least for all the infants she helped usher into the world, she was fully present if only for the weeks it took for their mothers to recover. It had been worth it, she thought. To feel so needed, so important. She thought about how it felt when an exhausted mother, with her help, was able to get the hungry newborn to latch to her breast. She thought about the sense of satisfaction she had when each holiday card arrived, photos of those infants growing up before her eyes. It made her feel that her work mattered.

Something pricked at her as she descended the steep stairwell to the subway at 14th Street. She couldn't put her finger on what it was. It had something to do with her mother. Something the psychic had said? It felt like the times lately when she'd forget a name or a word. Like an engine that wouldn't turn over, no matter how many times you turned the key and pumped the gas. The way fear would creep up and she'd worry that her mother's fate would be her own. Could her own mind possibly be failing her? Then finally, that old engine would rev: the word or name or memory returning.

But now, whatever was niggling at her eluded her.

The subway platform was empty save for a couple of teenaged boys who were looking at something on one of the boys' phones. A woman in a suit and heels sitting primly near the doors. Her heart immediately went out to her, this poor woman on Christmas Eve, dressed for a meeting.

On the train, she found a seat and studied the map. Four stops until Times Square, then a quick walk. But if she didn't get there on time, Simone could be on a train headed—anywhere— then what would happen? If Simone left the city? The state? How would they ever find her? What if they never did?

One of her clients lost a child once. Sofia had put that tragedy away in the vault of her memory: the dark, locked place that held all the disasters: the stillbirths and near-deaths. The one mother who didn't make it. She'd been called by a former client for whom she had been a doula about five years before. She was pregnant again and hoped that Sofia could be with her through this birth, as well.

"Of course. And how is Pia? She must be so excited to be a big sister!"

The mother had paused before drawing in a heartbreaking, shuddering breath.

The little girl had wandered away when the family was on a beach vacation. The mother, exhausted, had fallen asleep on the warm sand. The father had not been paying attention, assuming that the mother was watching her. It took an entire week before they found her body.

Sofia had not been able to sleep that night, thinking about how easy it is to lose someone. About the horror that poor mother must have felt when her daughter disappeared. She thought of those empty hours. The helplessness she must have felt. The guilt.

Now, she thought of her mother, like a child, wandering onto a train. She considered, again, all the terrible things that could happen to her.

When the train arrived at Times Square, her legs felt leaden as she made her way up the stairs.

At least the freezing rain had stopped, the air warmed a bit. The sky felt heavy. It might snow. She clutched the red umbrella in her hand and made her way across 42nd Street.

Alex

The days were so short now, the sky beginning to dim in the late afternoon. Lately, she and Zu-Zu would get to the studios before the sun rose and not leave until after the sun set. It felt sometimes as if they had no lives outside of ballet. Together, they would make their way back to their apartment, bodies exhausted, brains taxed, and collapse onto the couch. They would ice their feet and watch TV, nodding off and realizing their toes had gone numb.

She had promised Zu-Zu that she would meet her at Lincoln Center, after the matinee, but now, she knew that if she did, she'd never do what she needed to do.

She pulled out her phone to check the Metro-North's holiday schedule. There was a train leaving for Danbury at 5:00 p.m. Not enough time to go to her apartment first to pack. Not even enough time to go back and say goodbye to Zu-Zu. But maybe that was a good thing. If she saw Zu-Zu, she knew she might not be able to make herself leave.

She thought about texting her mother, explaining what had really happened. At least this way, she'd be prepared when

Alex arrived at the train station at home. And maybe, because it was Christmas Eve, it would temper her disappointment. Her anger.

Instead, she ducked under an awning and texted her dad.

Daddy, she said, as if she were nine instead of nineteen. **Remember that time we went sledding?**

And she recollected the breathlessness as they climbed the hill. The way she hadn't worried about getting hurt. Hadn't worried about anything at all. She'd just lain down on that sled and stared up at the glorious sky. And she remembered the rush of freedom as she flew down the hill.

Was this what she wanted? Freedom?

Freedom from what? From ballet? She didn't even know what that would look like. Feel like. But, she thought, maybe ballet wasn't the problem at all. What if she wanted freedom from something bigger? From her mother's expectations? It sounded silly as she thought it. But in the end, isn't this why she'd walked off stage last night?

Zu-Zu had asked what she was thinking in that moment onstage when her body stopped. She remembered now. When the recycled snow began to fall from above, she had thought that if she were to walk out now—here, in front of thousands of people—she wouldn't have to make the choice later. Someone else, Nicholai, would make that choice for her.

She shivered outside Grand Central Terminal, her fingers numb with cold as she pulled her phone from her bag. Her dad had answered with a **?** She opened up the text thread with her mom and started to type.

Simone

Christmas Eve, 1968

Simone had woken on Christmas Eve morning to the sound of Steven snoring next to her. It was like music, she thought. A funny lullaby. She rolled over onto her side to look at him, at his sweet face, his long eyelashes pressed against the tops of his cheeks. She would never get tired of this. It would never grow old.

She slowly lifted the crocheted afghan, the one her grandmother had made for her, and quietly slipped out of the twin bed where they slept together, curled around each like tangled vines each night. The studio apartment too small for a full-size bed. She would miss these days, she thought, when they could afford a bigger place, a proper bed to sleep in.

Quietly, she walked across the parquet floor, tiptoeing so as not to wake him, and carefully opened the drawer where she kept her meager selection of clothes. She had only been able to bring a single suitcase with her to New York. It was all she was allowed to carry on the train. Plus, she'd left in haste. Her parents weren't happy about her leaving Boston. After she finished at Berklee, they had urged her to come home to Vermont and teach. But the idea of being stuck in a stuffy music room with a bunch of fourth graders blowing into plastic recorders was not her idea of a life. Of course, she had adored her own music teacher. Mrs. Mallory. She'd quietly and secretly thought of her as Mrs. Marshmallow, because she was so soft: her body, her sweet soprano. Her kindness. But she had been sad, too; Simone could see that even as a little girl. Mrs. Mallory should have been singing on stages all over Europe. But instead, she was here, in the northeast corner of Vermont, teaching a bunch of kids how to sing "Row, Row, Row Your Boat" in rounds. It was Mrs. Mallory who had pulled Simone into a hug at the end of fifth grade, when Simone was headed off to junior high. "You have a gift," she had said to her.

She had carried that kindness, that reminder, with her all through junior high school. She liked to sing, but she also loved the stringed instruments: cello, viola, violin. She had pleaded with her parents to buy her a cello, but it was too expensive. Too awkward to get onto the school bus. And so, her father had found a secondhand violin for her. The bow was warped, and it was a little too large for her at twelve years old.

In high school, it became clear that she would need a new instrument, and she saved every dime from a summer spent scooping ice cream to purchase the used Stradivarius copy. And it was on this instrument that she learned to play, *really* learned to play. It was the instrument she played for the Berklee audition. She'd had to take a bus to Boston, staying with a girlfriend who was studying at Emerson. And it was this instrument that she had put in her closet, when her parents said that they couldn't afford to send her to the conservatory. That she could study music at the state university while she got her degree in education. But she had been determined, applied for scholarships, and worked waiting tables all through school to pay her own tuition. And instead of going home after graduation, she'd bought

204 / *Tammy Greenwood*

a one-way ticket to New York City, and had carried her beloved violin with her.

It was in New York that she'd met Steven, at that club on Bleecker. And they had danced as Barbara Lewis sang, "Baby, I'm Yours." Afterwards, she'd asked him for a cigarette, and sweaty and breathless, they had stepped out onto the street to smoke, but instead, he'd dropped to one knee. "Until the stars fall from the sky," he had said. That is how long he would love her.

She had to remind herself how hopeful she had felt that night. Like their whole lives were ahead of them. Here they were, after all, in *New York City*. But things were moving slowly. Steven had decided he should keep taking classes, and so he'd enrolled at The New School. He worked all day — he'd gotten a janitorial job at a theater on Broadway — and took classes at night. Meanwhile, she was practicing. Practicing and playing for loose change all around the city. To her, it seemed like a pretty good deal, to get paid to play. Though between the two of them, they barely made enough to eat.

Sometimes when she was busking, people would hand her leftovers: slices of pizza or aluminum foil swans with bits of fancy food inside: filet mignon or, once, a whole lobster tail. She and Steven had sat at their tiny kitchen table and pretended they were at the Ritz-Carlton, dipping that lobster tail into melted margarine.

She wondered, of course, how long they would have to pay their dues. How long before she found her way into a chair in the symphony rather than the subway. How long before one of Steven's funny, charming pieces was scooped up. It was only a matter of time; of this, she was sure. And whenever she doubted that, she remembered Mrs. Mallory, her breath smelling of wintergreen candies: "You have a gift."

This morning, after she was dressed, she found her way to the attic room upstairs. Had they always had an attic room? That was peculiar. But up here, she found her violin case and

Steven's desk. She would leave him a note here, certain that he would find it at his desk.

She lifted the piece of stationery from a box, traced the white creamy paper with her finger, her heart singing at the sight of his initials, the same as her own, a bit of serendipity, she had thought. She had no idea he had such fancy paper. It must be for letters to the various directors and producers with whom he corresponded about his work.

She used his good pen, as well, to write the note that she hoped wouldn't reveal too much. It was a surprise, after all.

Darling, she said. *I've gone to pick up something special for Christmas. Don't follow me. It's a surprise.*

Yours until the stars fall from the sky,
Simone

Downstairs, she found a coat on the rack, a beautiful black coat with red roses. It must belong to their friend, Serafina. She was always leaving her things behind when she came over for visits. Serafina was an actress. Her clothes were flamboyant and wonderful. Simone often borrowed the items she left behind, and as she walked down the street, she'd pretend she was someone else. A free spirit, like Serafina.

It was chilly outside, puffy bits of snow falling.

At the little Italian market on the corner, she waited for Gianni, the shop owner, to arrive. It was early. And Christmas Eve, to boot. She worried for a moment that he wouldn't be open today, but then saw him rounding the corner, blowing warm air into his cupped hands. His eyes lit up when he saw her.

"*Ma buongiorno, bellissima!*" he hollered from nearly a block away. Gianni was a terminal flirt. Though it was harmless; he was old enough to be her father. His son, Giuseppe, was her age; he worked at the meat and cheese counter on the weekends, the spitting image of his father.

"After you," Gianni said, and winked, holding the door open for her as she entered the shop.

"Where are you headed today?" he asked her. "On Christmas Eve?"

"I have to meet someone," she said. She looked at the clock above the counter. It was eight o'clock. "And I'm running late."

"It will take me just a minute to make you an espresso. Can you wait?"

"Of course," she said.

She reached into the pocket of the coat and realized that her wallet had been in her other jacket.

Gianni saw her struggling.

"No, no," he said, as if he had never intended to charge her. "It is my gift to you," he said.

"*Grazie*," she said, kissing him on the cheek. "*Buon Natale!*" she said as she left the shop, the sleigh bells tinkling behind her.

Sofia

As Sofia walked along 42nd Street, she figured she'd quickly check Bryant Park first, just in case the psychic had meant 89 *West* 42nd Street. It certainly would make things easier if her mother was simply sitting on a park bench rather than on her way to God-knows-where on a train out of Grand Central.

It seemed only locals, searching for last-minute gifts, were on the streets. It reminded her of shopping with her mother in the city, searching for dresses to wear for upcoming tours. Her mother's closet was an odd mix of blue jeans and gowns. There was very little in between, because she was always either performing or lounging around the house. The dresses were all black. Formal, but simple. They often were sleeveless; her mother explained that she preferred a bare shoulder upon which to hold her instrument. Fabric created a barrier between her and the feeling of her instrument. She explained that her violin was, essentially, an extension of herself. Another limb.

As they perused the racks of gowns at Saks, Sofia had been drawn to a beautiful green dress with a sequined bodice and swirl of chiffon; she thought it looked like a Christmas tree.

Festive. And it would match her mother's green eyes and the beautiful emerald earrings Sofia's father had given her last year.

"Mama," she had said to the door behind which her mother was changing.

"There's a pretty green one out here. You should try it."

Her mother had opened the door, just a crack, and poked her head out.

Sofia held the dress in her arms, folded over so it wouldn't brush the floor.

"Oh, Sofia," she said. "It is lovely. But we have a dress code."

"What's a dress code?" she had asked.

"Like a uniform," she'd explained.

The word *uniform* made Sofia think of police officers and firemen. Of soldiers. The thought of her mother high-stepping alongside a hundred other identical women in identical black dresses made her giggle.

"You know what? I think you're right. And won't they all be surprised when I show up in my beautiful green dress?"

She had no idea if her mother actually wore the dress, but for a moment, it had felt as if they were conspiring with each other.

Sofia realized that these moments of connection with her mother, though few, were like bolts of electricity when she remembered them. The times when they understood each other felt magical, but they also made the times when she was gone even more painful. She longed for the simple moments when she and her mother shared things: a decadent piece of cake from William Greenberg Desserts, an exasperated sigh as they stood waiting for a train on a hot day, a secret kept from her father. When her mother was away, those brief moments of connection felt like a dream. She didn't want much, only this.

But now, here she was. Alone with her mother nearly every moment of every day, and she still felt as far away from her as she had growing up.

Was it possible to lose your mother a hundred times?

Feeling a renewed sense of purpose, Sofia walked briskly along the edge of the nearly empty park. By the time she arrived at Grand Central Terminal, she had to bend over, hands pressed to her knees, as she tried to catch her breath.

Her phone buzzed in her pocket. A call.

"Hi, Sofia, this is Deputy Commissioner O'Hara again. We got a call that a woman matching your mother's description is in Grand Central Terminal, in the main concourse. We've dispatched an officer; his name's Hayes. Should be there soon. But if you're close, you might want to meet him there."

"Thank you!" she said. "I'll be there."

Inside the train station, Sofia's eyes searched the main lobby and fell on the gorgeous golden clock at the center of the room. The clock.

The psychic had been right!

Unlike the streets outside, the terminal was crowded with people. She thought, again, of the trains departing and was overwhelmed. She needed to get to her mother, and quickly. Her eyes scanned the crowded concourse, searching for that black coat with the red roses. Where was she?

But then, beyond the din of the travelers, she heard music. Faint at first, but growing louder.

Tears filled her eyes.

She pushed through the crowd, toward the sound of the music, and stopped when she saw that an audience had gathered in a circle on the balcony overlooking the concourse.

Alex

When Alex reached Grand Central Terminal, the sun had already set; the rain had turned to snow again, the air scattered with icy filaments.

Where are you? Zu-Zu texted, and Alex felt her shoulders sink. But she knew that if she saw Zu-Zu, she would fall apart. Change her mind.

She texted back. **Going to catch the train home. I'll come back after Christmas to get my stuff. I'm sorry, Zee.**

There was nothing for a moment, but then the bubble appeared as Zu-Zu drafted her text.

I love you, A.

She had nothing with her but her dance bag, of all things. The pointe shoes nestled in their mesh sack inside.

She stood outside the station, looking up at the snow, letting the cold flakes land on her cheeks, on her eyelashes.

The station was decorated for the holiday, and as she entered through the glass doors on Lexington, she felt enveloped in warmth. She walked through the Holiday Market, her eyes stinging as she spied the *Nutcracker* snow globe display. She gingerly picked up a snow globe with a ballerina in arabesque inside.

"It's beautiful, isn't it?" the woman at the kiosk said, nodding approvingly at her selection. "Oh! You're a dancer."

Alex felt her heart plummet. Was she anymore? And if not, what was she? *Who* was she?

"It plays music, too," the woman said, gesturing to the snow globe.

Alex picked it up and turned the brass key on the bottom. "Waltz of the Snowflakes" played as snow fell all around the dancer inside.

Oddly, the music inside the Snow Globe echoed, as though it were playing twice. But that wasn't possible. Maybe there was a second music box? She glanced around, then looked at the woman, confused. But that other "Waltz" was coming from somewhere else.

"Thank you," Alex said, returning the globe to the display, and kept walking toward the main concourse.

As she approached the beautiful golden clock at the center of the cavernous lobby, the music got louder. Someone was *playing* the "Waltz of the Snowflakes." The haunting music beckoned her, and once again, she was in the wings, waiting, her heart pounding with anticipation.

She turned right and hobbled along toward the stone stairwell to the east balcony that overlooked the main concourse. The brass railing gleamed in the warm Christmas lights. She limped up the stairs, wishing she had a shoe so she could ditch this stupid boot.

The overhead speaker announced the modified schedule for the holiday. The last Metro-North train would be departing in only fifteen minutes. The music beckoned her.

At the top of the balcony, a small crowd congregated, clutching cups of coffee, checking their phones, and the departure and arrival schedules. And under the giant arched windows was the old woman she had seen on the bus.

The woman had removed her coat, and stood in a beautiful green gown, her violin at her shoulder. Her silver hair, spun into two braids atop her head, glimmered in the lights. Her eyes closed, she plucked out those staccato notes, conjuring a snowstorm with her bow.

When the violinist opened her eyes, she looked far away. But as she gazed across the balcony, she saw Alex, and her eyes lit up with recognition. She pulled her bow away from her instrument and beckoned Alex to come closer.

And Alex looked at her, eyes filled with tears, and nodded.

Alex quickly undid the Velcro straps from the boot, kicking it to the side. She sat on the floor and put on her pointe shoes, tying the ribbons snugly around each ankle. She pulled off her coat and unwrapped her scarf and moved to the center of the balcony. "Excuse me," she said to a man on his phone. "Pardon me," she said to a young mother who was trying to calm her fussy baby.

Alex moved into position, the position she had been in last night. But now, she closed her eyes, saw the snow swirling around her. Saw her father waiting for her to fly down the hill. She felt something ancient in her body, the memory of the music. The memory of the way she had felt the first time she watched the dancers perform when she was a little girl. The buzzing hum of it. That beautiful thrum.

The woman began to play the piece from the beginning; the tentative notes sounded like she was asking permission. Offering an invitation.

And she danced. Cautiously at first—the floor was a bit slippery—and the crowd was not aware of what was happening. But as the music swelled, her body became expansive. The music filling her up.

Soon, the people who had been caught in their own worlds,

in this in-between place, had pressed to the edges of the balcony to give her space. Those who had been on their phones now held them up, recording her.

But she was hardly aware of the Christmas travelers, the mothers and fathers, the businessmen and women, the families. She was only aware of her body and the music, and the beauty she was making with it.

This was her gift. And, one last time, she wanted to share it.

Sofia

Sofia saw the police officer at the foot of the stairs to the east balcony. He was tall and thin, in his twenties. His cheeks and nose were red, like a child who'd been playing out in the snow too long.

"Excuse me?" she said. "Are you Officer Hayes?"

He nodded, surprised.

"It's my mom," she said, explaining. "The one you're searching for. The silver alert?"

"Oh!" the kid said. "Oh, that's great. We got a call that she's up there. On the balcony."

As he spoke, he seemed even younger. Of course, this poor guy would be on duty on Christmas Eve. She wondered if he had a family waiting for him at home. If he was old enough to have children of his own yet.

"My grandma has dementia, too," he said as they climbed the stairs together. "She lives with us now. Me and my dad."

Oh, man. He was such a baby, still living at home.

At the top of the stairs, there was a wall of people, and the sound of a violin filled the concourse with its aching beauty.

Sofia pushed through the crowd, mumbling her apologies. Then she saw what everyone was looking at.

Her mother stood in the center alcove, in an emerald dress, the empty violin case at her feet. The instrument was propped on her shoulder, cradled by her delicate chin, and with eyes closed, she cast a spell with her music.

But what was this? In the middle of the balcony, a young woman, wearing pointe shoes, was dancing. In blue jeans and a fuzzy white sweater, her hair loose, she appeared to be lost inside the music. They were *both* lost inside the music. The entire crowd was silent, hushed by the beauty of this, by the magic of this.

Sofia felt a shiver run through her. "Waltz of the Snowflakes" was her mother's favorite piece from *The Nutcracker Suite*. Simone had tried to explain the genius of it to Sofia. Sofia listened but couldn't really understand what she was saying about the way the notes replicated the randomness of snow falling. It had felt like her mother was speaking a foreign language.

But now, here, the music was the only language. Translated by this lovely dancer.

The officer stood next to her and removed his cap, holding it to his chest. She felt her heart come unhinged at the odd gesture of reverence.

"That's her?" he whispered. "Your mom?"

She nodded but couldn't find the words to explain that until this moment, she hadn't understood. She hadn't thought beyond her own needs being unmet. Her own loneliness and aching want for her mother. She hadn't been able to see that her mother's calling, this gift, was bigger than she.

Breathless, the dancer spun a web of her mother's music, the intricate design of a snowflake crafted from the single notes played one after another. Until, like the hush after a snowstorm, it was over.

Simone

She'd come to Grand Central Terminal to make the recording for Steven for Christmas. They had barely enough money to pay the rent, and so they'd promised each other they would be creative. She expected that Steven would write her a song. He'd been staying up late every night for a week, and had covered the piece of sheet music he'd been doodling on when she came into the room.

Their friend Henry worked for a recording studio and had access to a reel-to-reel that would create a good recording. She'd been practicing the arrangement she'd made of "Baby, I'm Yours" whenever Steven was at work.

When the doctor confirmed what she already suspected, she thought, *what a beautiful way to break the news.* She'd play their song and, after the music, tell him he'd need to wait until next summer to get the rest of his gift. Their baby.

She hadn't really thought about being a mother before. She hadn't played with dolls when she was young. She'd only ever babysat twice, both times ending in disaster (once when she set off the smoke alarm making popcorn, and once when the little girl wet her parents' bed). She'd allowed the girl to convince her to sleep there instead of in her own room. She didn't know the first thing about babies.

But somehow, when the nurse told her, she hadn't been afraid or upset. Instead, she'd thought of Steven. Steven with his kindness and patience. She'd seen the way he was with his younger sisters, all three of them. How he was with the puppy they'd been tasked with dog-sitting when their friend went out of town. She'd watched, mesmerized, as he sat and colored in a coloring book for hours with his youngest sister, Margaret. And how he'd patiently cleaned up accident after accident the puppy made on their floor.

It was Steven she thought of when the nurse gauged her reaction to the news. Simone must have looked both stunned and scared, because the nurse had looked at her with a mix of curiosity and preemptive compassion.

It was Steven she thought of as she walked home that cold afternoon. About the fact that there was no one else in the world that she would rather have a baby with.

When she thought of her music, her career, of course, she knew this would waylay things. But delaying and derailing were two different things. And she knew that Steven would never expect her to abandon her dreams. That together, they would make a family, but they would also keep making music.

This Christmas gift would be one he would remember forever. The beginning of everything.

But when she stepped off the bus at Grand Central Terminal, she had walked down the steps onto the cold street and remembered. Steven was gone. It was like this: fog clearing from a quiet lake. The clarity of who she was, of where she was, of *when* she was, emerging like the sun from behind a wall of clouds.

She felt the hem of her dress dragging on the wet sidewalk,

and lifted it. Why was she wearing this green gown? The one Sofia had picked out for her all those years ago? And why was she carrying her violin to the train station? Was she traveling? Was she leaving her family, again, at Christmas?

It had never gotten easier—leaving them. Leaving Sofia. Her daughter's eyes so filled with sadness every time she pulled her suitcase from the closet. The hurt in Sofia's voice every time Simone spoke to her from a pay phone.

She knew Sofia was being cared for by Steven. That was one thing she had gotten right. But what she hadn't anticipated was the hole she would leave behind.

The sky had grown dark.

And she was twenty-four again, in her borrowed coat, on Christmas Eve. Going to the most beautiful train station in the most beautiful city—her city—to play.

She went straight to the east balcony. The golden clock at the center of the concourse stood below like a beacon. It said 4:30. But that couldn't be right. It was 6:00 a.m. when she left the apartment, left Steven sleeping. And she'd come straight here.

Or had she? She remembered seeing Gianni at his shop, getting her espresso. She remembered the scent of fresh bread.

She had come straight here; she was supposed to meet Henry at seven o'clock. He would bring the reel-to-reel and make the recording.

But where was he?

She thought about the bus ride here. Every day since they got to the city, she gathered her instrument and rode the bus. Each day, she found a place to play her music. And every night, she scoured the paper for auditions. But until she got a job, it was the music that mattered. And Mrs. Mallory had known all those years ago that music was her gift.

The gift. Yes, that was why she had come. To make the gift for Steven.

She removed her coat and set it on the floor behind her. She opened her violin case and pulled out the instrument.

And suddenly, she was in the orchestra pit at Teatro Colón, at La Scala, at Palais Garnier. All at once.

On the stage above, she could hear the hushed sound of the dancers' feet as they stilled, the brush of the curtains as they opened.

And she began.

When she saw the girl, her eyes wild with recognition, with sorrow, with hope, it was Sofia she thought of. Could this be Sofia? But what had happened to her foot?

No. Sofia was at home with her father. They planned to have waffles for Christmas breakfast and, later, go see a matinee. She had talked to them last night. When she'd hung up, it had felt like she'd swallowed the moon.

No, this girl was not Sofia. She was one of the dancers. And so, she had stopped playing and waited for her to be ready.

Then, there was only the music.

Alex

The sound of the applause pulled her back into the world. Back into Grand Central Terminal, back into her body, back into this moment in time. Where had she gone?

Her limbs buzzed, her heart pounding against her ribs as she caught her breath. Around her, the makeshift audience of people had put their phones down and were clapping and smiling. A little girl in a white coat twirled around with her arms over her head, on her tippy-toes.

And she felt something move inside her, shifting. *Lifting*.

She recalled an old memory, one she'd somehow forgotten.

She was eleven years old, and she was cast as Clara in *The Nutcracker*. The auditions had been nerve-racking, but her mother had rubbed her back and told her to relax, to trust her body. And it had worked. She kept making cut after cut after cut, until it was just her and one other girl left. And when the other girl was dismissed, she had burst into tears. It had made Alex's chest ache. She knew that she was lucky to have been chosen; usually the role went to one of the older girls. But it didn't feel like she'd won anything at all.

Rehearsals were so awful. The older girls wouldn't speak to her. The younger ones, either. But at home, it was all her mother could talk about, telling anyone who would listen. During rehearsals, her mom sat outside the studio, her face expectant and proud, as she watched Alex rehearse. She took videos with her phone through the glass, thinking she was being discreet, and then posted them to Facebook. Alex knew she was proud, but it felt like too much. All of it.

She wanted to quit. She wanted to just tell her teacher that she wasn't ready; that they should let her understudy take the role. But it would have crushed her mother. She could already imagine her crestfallen expression. Her silence that was louder than any words she could offer.

So she had kept going, dragging herself to class and rehearsals. Ignoring the whispers of the girls. Ignoring the heaviness in her chest. What choice did she have?

When opening night came, she got ready alone backstage while the other girls giggled nervously, growing quiet when she walked by. She stretched in the wings, feeling completely alone.

The party scene was a blur. There was so much going on onstage, so many characters. Someone dropped their doll, and the boy playing Fritz missed a cue. But within what felt like moments, it was over. Backstage, she slipped into the nightgown for the dream sequence, and she went onto the stage.

In this scene, she was alone. She was out there on the stage with only the music. The clock. And as the orchestra played, something happened. Alex disappeared. And she *was* Clara . . . knee-deep in the fog that rolled across the stage. The glowing clock striking midnight. The Christmas tree growing until it towered over her. She was so small here.

And the music carried her through the snowy world of the Snow Queen. But as she climbed into the carriage that would

222 / Tammy Greenwood

take her to the Land of the Sweets, and the audience roared with applause, and the curtain fell, she had only felt—*lost*.

Now, she gazed, breathless, at the faces of the people in the train station. She looked at the woman with the violin, who nodded at her knowingly. And knew what she needed to do.

Sofia

When it was over, when the music ended, when the impromptu performance was done and the crowd had dispersed, her mother looked like a sleepwalker woken from a dream.

Sofia caught her eye from across the balcony and smiled. Waved. "Mom!!"

"She's okay?" the police officer asked.

"She is," she said.

"Do you want me to call a paramedic, to make sure?" he asked.

She shook her head. "No. She's fine."

"Alrighty, then," he said. "You and your mom have a Merry Christmas. I'll make sure the alert gets canceled."

"Thank you," she said.

She walked quickly across the stone balcony to her mother, who stood still, her violin in one hand, bow in the other.

The dancer sat on a bench and was removing her pointe shoes. She looked up at Sofia for a moment and smiled, a wide-eyed grin. A joyful, breathless happiness.

"Thank you," Sofia said. "What a beautiful gift."

The girl shook her head. "No. It was a gift to me," she said. "Her music. It made me remember something."

Remember.

"Mom," Sofia said as she approached her mother.

"Sofia," Simone said. Recognition. Lucidity.

"That was breathtaking," Sofia said. "And you're wearing the dress I picked out."

"I am indeed," she said, as if noticing it for the first time. "I always wear it on Christmas Eve."

"You do?" Sofia asked, tears stinging, feeling awash in that same strange longing. That yearning for what she had never had. *Saudade.* But here she was, with everything she'd longed for in front of her. She might not have much time, but they had some.

She reached out for her mother's free hand, which was soft and delicate in her own. She remembered the way it felt that day in Milan, when her mother had held her hand and yelled at those boys.

"I saw your note. To Daddy."

"Daddy's gone," Simone said, her eyes gentle and teary.

"Yes," she said, and squeezed her hand. "It's just you and me, Mom."

Sofia helped Simone put her instrument back into the case. She held her elbow as they descended the winding staircase that led down to the concourse.

That golden clock towered, like Cinderella's clock striking midnight. She wondered when the spell would lift. When the confusion would return. When the magic of what had happened here would turn to dust.

Outside, the snow was coming down in furious swirls now. There were taxis lined up along the curb, and Sofia hailed one.

"We should get home, Mom," she started. But when she turned back, her mother was staring up into the night sky.

"It's like our song," she said. "The stars falling from the sky."

"It is," she said.

"I'm going to be a mother," she said. "I just found out."

Sofia thought of the mothers she'd helped, each one bearing the same expression in those moments when life began. Fear of the unknown, yes—every single time—but also joy.

"You're going to be a *good* mom," Sofia said. It was the only gift she had to give her.

Alex

Alex collapsed onto the seat on the train, her body buzzing from the performance in the train station. She closed her eyes and leaned her head against the seat rest.

In her pocket, her phone vibrated.

Probably her mother. She ignored it.

It buzzed again, then again and again.

Taking a deep breath, she pulled it out and glanced at the screen. Twenty alerts. Texts. Calls. Instagram. Twitter. Snapchat. Her phone was alive in her hands, buzzing like a bee.

Probably just people wishing her a Merry Christmas?

She opened the text from Zu-Zu first. **ALEX!**

Attached was a link to a video. She clicked on it, confused. Muffled noises, the back of someone's head. Then, her. The sound of the woman's violin was tinny. She retrieved her Air-Pods from her purse and put them in.

And she watched herself. Watched what it was that everyone had seen. It was like watching a movie. She felt herself swoon at the beauty of it. Of the beauty she and the old woman were making together. When it ended, the tears came harder. And her body trembled.

Text after text after text. The number of video views going up and up and up. There were at least ten different videos, from ten different vantage points. MIRACLE ON 42nd STREET? one said.

She watched them all, then set the phone, still vibrating, on the empty seat next to her. She closed her eyes and dreamed herself back onto that improvised stage. When the phone buzzed again, she looked down.

Ulyana.

She wiped her tears and studied the text.

Saw the video. Please come home. After the break. I will speak to Nicholai.

Alex felt her chest heave. She had a choice to make. She was getting a second chance, a *final* chance, maybe.

She picked up the phone and started to respond to Ulyana.

Thank you.

But then, with trembling fingers, she continued:

I appreciate this, but I am going to take some time to figure out what I really want. Who I am. Merry Christmas to you and Nicholai.

Next, she texted her mother:

On my way home. Can you pick me up at the train station? The train gets into Danbury at 9:00.

Her mother answered right away.

Of course. Are you okay?

She double-clicked the text with a thumbs-up. Because she *was* okay. She was better than okay. She knew this conversation was going to be hard, that her mother might not understand right away. She might not ever understand. But she was nineteen now. Nearly twenty. And, like Zu-Zu was always saying: she could do hard things.

She powered her phone down, put it in her bag, and looked out the window, imagining all the places she could go. All the dreams she might pursue. All the other gifts she might have to share.

Simone

Christmas Day

In the morning, Simone awakens to snow lacing the windows. In the kitchen, she hears Steven shuffling across the floor as he makes breakfast. Homemade struffoli, his mother's recipe. She can hear him humming a tune, one of the songs he's been working on.

She rolls over, her breasts tender, her body feeling as heavy as lead. She could stay here all day until the world is covered in white.

She could listen to the sounds of her husband in the Christmas kitchen.

But she has a gift to give him.

Henry had given her the reel-to-reel tape, and she wrapped it in silver foil, with a red ribbon.

She's going to be a mother, she thinks. In a year, they will be a family. In a year, they will be three.

She pulls herself from bed and puts on her robe. She slips on her slippers and yawns.

The whole apartment smells like coffee and bacon and the sweet smell of the struffoli.

When he sees her in the kitchen doorway, he sets down the spatula he has in one hand and beckons for her to come to him.

She has the gift in her hand. She offers it to him without a word. He unwraps it carefully, something he will do with a hundred other gifts over the next fifty years. It is excruciating, the way he prolongs the anticipation. It will drive Sofia crazy with exasperation. "Daddy," she'll say. "Just open it!!"

Sofia, she thinks.

It's Sofia standing at the kitchen stove. Sofia with a spatula in her hand, a smile on her face.

"Good morning, sunshine!" Sofia says, just like her father used to.

"Good morning," Simone says.

She sees Steven in her daughter's face. In her calm and quiet demeanor. She helps women when they have babies, she remembers. Her patience and calm make her good at this. That is her father's gift to her.

"You're famous," Sofia says. "Someone recorded your performance at Grand Central yesterday. It's all over the Internet."

She's confused. She thinks about the nearly empty train station when she played the song for Steven. When she said, "You're going to be a Daddy!" into the microphone.

Everything is messy; time feels loose. Weak. And so, she does what Constance has told her to do.

Touch something. Take a deep breath. Name something you can see, something you can hear, something you can smell, and something you can taste. Something you can touch.

Her daughter, at the stove.

The sound of Ella Fitzgerald on the stereo.

The scent of coffee.

The taste of the struffoli Sofia offers to her.

The feel of her hand. Her daughter. Right here.

Dear Reader,

First, a spoiler alert. If you have not read *Gifted*, please do before you read this letter.

This is the first Christmas story I have written. I have always thought that Christmastime in New York City is magical, and this story is, in many ways, a story about magic—or serendipity, at least.

The idea for *Gifted* first came to me after I saw a viral video on YouTube in which a little girl drops a coin into a street musician's hat, a simple act which sets into motion a flash mob's performance of Beethoven's Ninth Symphony, "Ode to Joy." The video, in which a crowd gathers as over a hundred musicians and singers assemble to create a full orchestra, overwhelms me with emotion every time I watch it. I wanted to capture this aching, beautiful feeling in fiction, but it has taken me ten years to do so.

Of course, the performance that occurs in my story is much smaller in scale—with only two performers: an elderly violinist and a young dancer. But my hope was to show a heartbreaking but life-affirming moment when two artists (at two very different places in their lives) collaborate to create a moment of grace.

Each of these women has complex and deep histories with their art. For Simone, her passion and commitment to her music has come at a cost, estranging her from her daughter. For Alex, her gift for dance has felt like a burden imposed upon her: her own mother's expectations and dreams leaving room for little else. The two strangers differ in many ways, but for a single, beautiful moment, they come together—each sharing their respective gift with the world one last time.

This is a story about mothers and daughters. About art and

ambition. Those of you who have read my work know that these are themes I return to again and again.

For the last four years, I have been mining the depths of my own experience raising a professional ballet dancer to write *The Still Point*, a novel about a pre-professional ballet conservatory and the mothers of the dancers who train there. *The Still Point* will be published in March of 2024. That novel further explores the dynamic between mothers and daughters as well as the themes of art and ambition that I touch on here. If you enjoyed *Gifted*, I think you will love *The Still Point*.

This book was a joy to write and I hope it brings you joy, as well.

Tammy Greenwood